SADDLE UP *for* STEAMBOAT

Allan Vaughan Elston

CENTER POINT LARGE PRINT
THORNDIKE, MAINE

This Center Point Large Print edition is published
in the year 2014 by arrangement with
Golden West Literary Agency.

The text of this Large Print edition is unabridged.
In other aspects, this book may vary
from the original edition.

Set in 16-point Times New Roman type.
ISBN: 978-1-62899-255-7
ISBN: 978-1-62899-256-4
Printed and bound by
www.printondemand-worldwide.com of Peterborough, England

Library of Congress Cataloging-in-Publication Data

Elston, Allan Vaughan, 1887–1976.
  Saddle up for steamboat / Allan Vaughan Elston. —
    Center Point Large Print edition.
  pages ; cm
  Summary: "Wayne Brady sets out to find the man who tried to frame
his best friend for murder"—Provided by publisher.
  ISBN 978-1-62899-255-7 (hardcover : alk. paper) —
  ISBN 978-1-62899-256-4 (pbk. : alk. paper)
  1. Large type books. I. Title.
  PS3509.L77S23 2014
  813'.52—dc23
                                                    2014028600

This book is made entirely of chain-of-custody materials

SADDLE UP
for
STEAMBOAT

I

It was thirty-three miles from Steamboat Springs to Slater Park, at the east edge of the Elkhead Mountains, and Dale Garrison didn't try to make it in one day. This was known as the Beef Trail, used in market season by the Reverse Four, the OVO, and other northern Routt County outfits. On this August day of the year 1901 the trail was deserted, and just after sundown Garrison came to Bart Conroy's cabin at the head of Mill Creek. No one was there, Conroy having hired out as a hay hand at the Cary Brothers' ranch on the Yampa River. But the latchstring was out. Garrison stopped and off-saddled for the night.

An hour after sunup he was on his way again, cutting just west of Quaker Mountain. He struck heavy timber at the head of First Creek. Again he saw no one. Garrison rode slowly, not gracefully, for he wasn't trained to the saddle. He was in fact a New Englander who'd come west only a year ago and who since then had idled about the Sheridan Hotel in Steamboat Springs, pretending to be on the lookout for a bargain in ranch property. A sham—because Dale Garrison had no intention of buying a ranch. Only a year ago in Connecticut, he'd finished serving a prison term for forgery. He had neither taste nor talent for the cattle business. His talent was for undercover dealings such as the one which had kept him profitably in Steamboat Springs for the past year.

Yet people might wonder how he could live so well there, indefinitely, without visible means of support. So to make himself plausible in the eyes of the town, he occasionally rode out to look at some ranch advertized for sale in a local weekly. He could always say it didn't quite suit him, or he could make a bid so low it was sure to be declined.

This trip was to the Mark Lassiter place in Slater Park. The ad said it was an improved half-section with Slater Creek running through it, surrounded by free-range forest land. It was known that Lassiter had already sold his cattle and now needed only to sell his land, and that all the Lassiter help had been laid off except one rider, Jim Gentry, who would himself be out of a job as soon as the ranch was sold.

Nothing in Dale Garrison's good-looking, clean-cut face suggested a man living by his wits. A year under the western sun had bronzed his skin, and since arriving in Colorado he'd worn the boots and hat of a westerner. His upper lip had a thin brown mustache, and his curling, brownish hair had deep sideburns. As an unattached male he'd been much in demand at social events around Steamboat. Mostly he'd kept politely aloof from them. The small-town life was boring him, and soon after making this sham inspection trip to

Slater Park he planned on spending a couple of weeks in Denver to taste the fleshpots there. It would mean riding a stagecoach seventy-five miles over the divide to Wolcott, and from there riding more than twice that far on a D. & R. G. train. After a couple of weeks in Denver he'd come back to Steamboat and pay another call on Abner Barnett.

He'd been calling on Barnett once every three months. Four calls a year on Abner Barnett, who owned the biggest general merchandise store in Routt County, should put him on Easy Street for life, he figured. But just for the looks of things, he must keep people thinking he was out scouting for a cow ranch.

The sun was mid-morning high when he crossed the head of Armstrong Creek at the edge of California Park. This was a high, open glade in the forest, and he supposed Slater Park would be something like it. After resting briefly he rode on. The ride was rougher than he'd expected; but in a way it should make him seem all the more sincere and plausible. For why would he ride this far to inspect a ranch unless he was really serious about buying it?

Garrison had a map of this trail, and by using it he identified landmarks. The two high, twin peaks off to the west would be the Bear's Ears. When he came to the fork of two tiny streams, the map told him they were Knowles and Circle

Creeks. Another hour should take him to Slater Park.

The sun was noon high when he came to the southerly end of it—an open space in the forest about two miles north and south by half a mile east and west. The streamlet meandering through it would be Slater Creek near its head. According to the map, the creek ran northwesterly past Columbus Mountain to join the Little Snake River near Slater post office on the Wyoming line.

Presently Garrison came to a rail fence with Lassiter's name over a gate there. Beyond he could see a log ranch house, a barn, and outcabins—with a pulley well midway between house and barn. Except for one horse in a corral no life was in sight. To Garrison's disappointment the house chimney showed no smoke. He'd counted on arriving just in time for a warm midday meal.

He moved on to the barn and off-saddled there. The corraled horse, he recognized as the one Mark Lassiter rode on shopping trips to Steamboat Springs. Absence of a second horse probably meant that the one hand, Jim Gentry, was away on some errand.

As he walked toward the house he saw that the front door stood open. No sound came from it. It was a sturdy house of lodgepole pine logs: four rooms, according to the ad in this week's *Steamboat Pilot*. The asking price for the ranch was $9000, and if Garrison made a bid at all, it would be for much less than that. Later he could say, and be confirmed by Lassiter, that he'd tried to buy the place and been turned down.

He stopped outside the door and called, "Anybody home?"

When no answer came, he began to sense that something was wrong. Looking in, he saw that the main room was empty. Then he saw that cabinet drawers had been pulled out and that a cushion had been ripped open. "Mr. Lassiter!" he called, and still got no answer.

He went in, crossed the main room, and looked into a combination dining room–kitchen. Something was more than wrong! Mark Lassiter was slumped forward over a table there. Blood stained his jacket and an open ledger on the table in front of him. Back of him was an open window. For a moment the shock transfixed Garrison; then he advanced fearfully to see if the ranchman still had life in him.

A close look and a touch told him that Lassiter was dead. The body was still warm, and the blood hadn't caked yet. It was blood from a bullet wound. The shot had come from behind, probably through the open window.

This room too had been searched, and the same, surely, would be true of the bedroom. Then Garrison remembered something he'd heard about Mark Lassiter. There'd been idle talk about it in the Sheridan Hotel lobby. Ten years ago the

11

failure of an Arizona bank had wiped out Lassiter's life savings. Since then he'd mistrusted banks. After resettling in Colorado he'd kept his estate in land and livestock, holding his cash to a minimum.

But the man had just sold two hundred steers, and rumour was that it was a cash deal. That many steers would have brought about six thousand dollars. More than likely, the money had never been banked—in which case Lassiter must have hidden it in some secret cache right here on the ranch.

Evidently the killer had thought so. He'd shot Lassiter and then searched the house. Probably he'd also searched the barn and outcabins.

Apparently the rancher had been sitting here, going over accounts in this open ledger. Garrison now saw that a page had been torn from the ledger. A blank page. And on it the dying man had scrawled a note in pencil. The note had blood on it, obscuring a word or two.

Garrison picked up the note and read it. It was a message to Jim Gentry, the only rider still employed here.

Jim:
    He shot from behind and I didn't see him. I passed out for a while. He's gone now. I guess he was hunting for my money and didn't find it. If I'm dead when you get back from

the U Bar, take the money to Judge Shumate at Hahn's Peak as part of my estate. There's a loose stone on the south side of the well coping. Look under it.

M. Lassiter

It would have been a painful effort for Lassiter, in the last minutes of his life, to write that message. Coming back to consciousness, he would need to wait till he heard the killer ride away. It couldn't have been long ago—possibly not more than an hour.

There was a chance that the killer had returned to the house after the note had been written. In that case he'd read it, followed its direction, and helped himself to the money.

Had he?

There was a simple way to find out. Garrison, always an opportunist, went outside and looked cautiously in all directions. Silence everywhere. No sign of a returning Jim Gentry. Often this past year, Garrison had studied a Routt County map; so he knew that the U Bar was on lower Slater Creek, just a few miles above Slater post office. A round trip there would take all day. So Jim Gentry wasn't likely to be back before sundown.

There was plenty of time to see whether or not the money was still under a stone of the well coping.

Garrison went quickly to the well. The side of it nearest the barn had a horse trough. The south side of it, nearest the house, didn't seem to have a loose stone. The coping was homemade masonry with foot-square slabs around the edges. Garrison examined the south side slabs one by one. At the barn he found a branding iron to pry with. When he used it, one of the slabs moved slightly. He pried it away and saw at once that the killer had failed to find what he'd been looking for.

The top of a small metal box was exposed there. After prying the box out, Garrison opened it and saw currency. The top package was of fifty-dollar bills, and he didn't bother to examine the rest. All in all, it was sure to be the price of two hundred mature steers plus whatever cash savings Lassiter had had on hand before the sale.

Garrison's first and natural impulse was to take the money and run.

Then he had a better idea. Better and much safer. He might have been seen riding this way; or he might meet someone on his ride back to Steamboat. It would put him under suspicion once the body was found. He'd be questioned and searched. The loot in his possession could convict him of a murder he hadn't committed.

So Garrison left the money—all of it—right there and replaced the coping stone. He withdrew from the well empty-handed. Back at the house, he circled to the side of it opposite from the well.

Looking in that direction, he spotted a boulder about two feet in diameter. He walked to it, counting his steps. Ninety paces. At the barn he found an irrigation shovel and with it returned to the boulder. Heaving mightily, he rolled the boulder a few feet to one side.

On the spot where it had rested he dug a hole a foot or so deep. He dropped the shovel by the hole and went back to the house.

There, at a kitchen table over which a dead man had collapsed, Dale Garrison made use of his talent as a professional forger.

It was a simple matter to erase nine pencilled words from the note. The words: "stone on the south side of the well coping."

Before replacing them with other words, Garrison practiced on scratch paper, not only to carefully imitate Lassiter's unsteady scrawl but also to select words which would approximately fill the erased space. As a skilled forger he'd made a career of imitating another man's writing. When he was done, the substituted words seemed definitely to be Lassiter's. He didn't need to forge the signature, because it was already there.

The final sentence of the message to Jim Gentry now read: ". . . There's a loose boulder ninety paces northeast of the house; look under it."

Garrison dropped the note on the table and burned the paper he'd practiced on.

Minutes later, he'd saddled up and was riding

southeasterly down the trail toward Steamboat Springs. If stopped and searched, nothing would be found on him. No loot; no gun. Dale Garrison didn't even own a gun. Wits, not guns, were the tools of his trade. Let the money lie for weeks, months if necessary, under a stone of a well coping. Whoever found the body would read the note. Inevitably he'd pace ninety steps in a specified direction and see a boulder which had been pushed aside for the digging of a hole. An empty hole, fresh-dug, with a spade lying by it.

Which would make it seem obvious that someone had read the note, followed its directions, helped himself to the money, and made off with it. It would all be reported to lawmen at Hahn's Peak, the county seat, who'd conclude that there'd be no use searching other areas of the ranch yard for Lassiter's money. They'd be off searching for a thief, not for hidden money. The money could lie indefinitely exactly where Lassiter had hidden it—until, the hue and cry over, Dale Garrison in the dark of a night would pay a stealthy visit to that coping stone.

Meantime, he figured, after a quiet week in town, he'd better take his already planned trip to Denver for some fun in the bright lights there. He could do some gambling at a few of the Holliday Street spots, and when he got back to Steamboat Springs he could claim a run of luck. It would plausibly explain his sudden affluence later on, when he'd heeled himself with the Lassiter money.

And there'd still be the Abner Barnett money, already flowing in at the rate of a thousand dollars per quarter.

Garrison rode on down the trail, past California Park and Quaker Mountain. One loose string of worry bothered him a little. The liveryman from whom he'd rented this horse would know he'd been gone from town two days. If asked where he'd been, he'd need a convincing answer.

The answer clicked when Garrison came to Bart Conroy's empty homestead cabin. He'd met Conroy only once, in a friendly poker game at the Sheridan Hotel. He remembered Conroy's mentioning that he'd spent five or six years cowboying in southern Idaho. *So I rode up to ask him about land prices there; and how Idaho compares with Routt County, Colorado, as a cattle country. He wasn't home. So I helped myself to a bunk for the night and then came back to town.*

That would be his answer, and no one could prove it wasn't true. Actually it *was* partly true, for he had ridden to Conroy's place and spent the night there. More likely, he wouldn't even be questioned.

Garrison continued on down the trail, passing Pilot Knob. Twice he heard riders coming and drew aside into the woods till they'd ridden by. When night came he rode on by starlight and

17

angled east until he struck the Hahn's Peak-Steamboat Springs stage road.

An hour after daybreak, he was eating breakfast at the Sheridan Hotel.

II

It was well past nightfall when a stagecoach left McCoy's, the first relay station out of Wolcott on the road to Steamboat Springs and Hahn's Peak. Of the nine passengers (three on each of the three seats), four had ridden a D. & R. G. train from Denver, transferring to this stage at Wolcott on the west slope of the Continental Divide. The trail was rock-strewn and rutty. The only one of the passengers who'd never ridden it before was Verna Bainbridge, from Ohio, on her way to Steamboat Springs to act as office secretary and housekeeper for an elderly bachelor uncle.

"How long will it take us," she asked, "to get there?"

Before the young cattle hand on her left could answer, the grizzled oldster on her right rattled off the full schedule of the run. "Eighteen hours from Wolcott to Steamboat, Miss, and another six hours on to Hahn's Peak. Puts us in Steamboat at noon tomorrow. We change teams four times between Wolcott and Steamboat—McCoy's, Topanah, Yampa, Yellowjacket Pass. Breakfast at Yampa. No stops 'cept to change horses and eat. Didn't usta be that way. Usta make two daylight runs of it with an overnight stop at Yampa."

The stock hand, Wayne Brady, got in a word. "This uncle of yours—he'll be meeting you?"

"No." She smiled at him through the veil which covered her face and hat. "He wrote saying he'd be attending court at Hahn's Peak for the next few days. I'm to stay at the Sheridan Hotel till he gets back."

"They serve right good grub there," the oldster put in. "It'll be the noon eatin' stop for this stage tomorrow. Then on north another twenty-eight miles to Hahn's Peak."

By now Verna knew that he was a retired stage driver named Walt Cody and that the cowboy on her left was on his way home after delivering a shipment of cattle to the Omaha stockyards. She'd met him on the train between Denver and Wolcott.

In the gloom of the coach the other passengers were only dim silhouettes. But she knew who they were because in the first few miles out of Wolcott, while it was still daylight, the talkative Walt Cody had identified them to her. The three on the middle seat, directly in front of her, were a Steamboat Springs banker named Milner, a Georgetown lawyer named Farr, and a strikingly handsome and well-dressed man named Dale Garrison.

Garrison also had been on the train with her from Denver. He hadn't approached her on the train, but at the stage depot in Wolcott he'd tipped his hat and introduced himself. "Been living there myself this past year," he'd told her on learning that she'd be putting up at the Sheridan Hotel until her lawyer uncle got back from attending district court at Hahn's Peak. "There's worse places. Anything I can do for you, let me know."

"You're in business there, Mr. Garrison?"

"Not yet, but soon, maybe. Figure on buying a stock ranch if I can find one that suits me. Been taking a little holiday in Denver, last couple of weeks. Looks like we're about ready to pull out." He'd tried to maneuver himself into a seat beside her on the stage, but somehow the Cary Brothers' cowboy, Brady, had outmaneuvered him.

All Verna could see of him now was the back of his well-shaped head. Milner and Farr, on either side of him, were already napping as the coach rocked along through the night.

The front seat trio were even dimmer, but the girl had been told who they were. Two were a Routt County deputy sheriff and his prisoner on their way to the Hahn's Peak jail. Verna had watched them board the coach, handcuffed wrist to wrist. The third front-seat passenger was an over-rouged and overdressed woman. "They call her Mattie," Walt Cody had confided in an undertone. "On her way to a dive in Brooklyn. Brooklyn's a row of saloons across the river from Steamboat. Ain't no saloons in Steamboat—they

20

got local option. Those hangouts across the river are outside the town limits. Plenty of hell-raisin' goes on over there."

They were climbing a grade now, the four-horse team moving at a walk. "It'll be a long night, Miss Bainbridge," Brady said. "Why don't you try to get a little sleep?"

"I'm too excited to sleep. Riding a stagecoach over a dark, mysterious mountain!" She smiled again at the cowboy on her left. "And please don't call me Miss. It sounds so formal. My name's Verna."

"Mine's Wayne," Brady told her. "I ride for the Cary outfit down around Hayden."

"You drove cattle to the railroad, then shipped them to Omaha?"

"Yeh, but we didn't come this way, we drove them north via Baggs to the Union Pacific at Rawlins, Wyoming. Longer, but no high mountain pass to go over that way. When we got 'em carred at Rawlins, the other riders went back to the ranch leading my horse. I rode the caboose to Omaha, and now I'm taking the shortest route home."

Verna raised her veil, now that they were in high country where showers had settled the dust. "That prisoner in the front seat!" she wondered, "what did he do?"

"They claim he stole horses from an Elk River outfit. Deputy Cal Westbrook caught up with him

21

at Aspen and is fetchin' him to the Hahn's Peak jail."

"Hahn's Peak? Is that a mountain or a town?"

"Both. It's really just a played-out mining camp, but in the old days it was the only settlement in the county. So they made it the county seat and it still is."

The swaying of the coach lulled Verna, and quite suddenly she was asleep. When she wakened the stage was changing horses at Topanah station.

Everyone except the saloon girl Mattie got off for a cup of coffee. The station master's wife was serving it. This time Dale Garrison out-maneuvered Brady and got two cups, handing one to Verna in order to pair himself with her. Deputy Sheriff Westbrook got cups for himself and his prisoner. When Brady was served, he joined Westbrook.

"Hi, Cal," Brady said. "Anything happen while I've been gone?"

"Depends on how long you've been gone, Wayne."

"Let's see. Took us ten days to push those steers from Hayden to Rawlins; three days on a U.P. stock train; a day to sell 'em and another day for me to take in the bright lights of Omaha; then two days on the way back home. Makes pretty near three weeks, Cal."

"Then I reckon you haven't heard about what happened in Slater Park."

"I sure haven't. What happened?"

"About three weeks ago a killer sneaked up and shot Mark Lassiter dead. Then he searched the place for Mark's money but couldn't find it. Just before Mark died he scrawled a note telling his man Jim Gentry where to find the money. Jim says he got home about sundown, found his boss dead, read the note, and went to the spot it named, but nothing was there except an empty hole. He figures somebody else read the note before he did and made off with the money."

"Have they got any suspects yet, Cal?"

"Yeh. One. Jim Gentry himself."

It shocked and outraged Brady. "I don't believe it. I've known Jim a long time. He's not the kind to sneak-shoot his own boss and then rob him."

"He's not charged with the shooting," the deputy said. "Only with helping himself to the money."

"You mean he didn't report the killing?"

"He reported it all right. Rode ten miles to Hahn's Peak and said he found his boss shot dead. Claims he followed the directions of the note and found an empty hole. Maybe he did; maybe he didn't."

"Where is he now?"

"If he didn't make bail, he's in jail at Hahn's Peak. His trial comes up day after tomorrow. He's not charged with murder, you understand; just grand theft."

Wayne Brady's coffee was bitter cold and he set

it aside. "They're loco—charging him like that. I'll stake my best horse and saddle he never stole a penny in his life."

"The state's case," Westbrook explained with a noncommital shrug, "is that he dug up the money —six or seven thousand dollars—and rode toward Hahn's Peak with the intention of turning it over to Judge Shumate like the note directed. But on the way temptation got too big for him. It would take a ranch hand ten or fifteen years to earn that much money. So they figure he hid it, maybe in a knothole or under a rock, then rode on to Hahn's Peak and told the sheriff he'd found Lassiter dead and the money cache empty."

Wayne had questions, but the deputy had no more details. "Been away myself this past week, chasin' a horse thief to Aspen."

By now everyone else was back on the coach, and Dale Garrison had used the opportunity to promote himself to a place beside Verna Bainbridge on the rear seat. The only empty space was between a banker and a lawyer on the middle seat. Brady was about to take it when the veteran Walt Cody saw his disappointed look.

"Reckon I'll ride up top with the driver, here to Yampa," Cody said. "Get some fresh air that way. You might as well take my place, young fella."

So Brady climbed in beside the girl with Garrison on the other side of her. A whip cracked and the stage rolled out for the next station, which would be the breakfast stop, Yampa.

With his mind fixed on Jim Gentry's trouble, Wayne for a while took no part in talk going on between his seatmates. The girl was asking, "How big a place is it?"

"Steamboat? Not big," Garrison told her. "Less than a thousand people. But it's the trading center for a whopper-size county. Goes clear to the Utah line; hundred and fifty miles one way by sixty miles the other. Two newspapers and five general stores. All Steamboat needs is a railroad. Won't be long till it gets one. They say a man named Moffatt . . ."

Garrison chattered on, and subconsciously Brady was aware that he was making a dead set for the girl, turning on the charm full blast. An hour ago, Brady would have resented it and cut in himself. Right now he was too preoccupied with worry about a friend caged in a crude Hahn's Peak jail, with a trial date only forty hours away.

"I just can't believe it!" he muttered audibly.

Verna heard, and turned her blonde head toward him. "You mean about Mr. Moffatt's railroad?"

"No. I don't believe Jim did it."

"Who's Jim?"

"A good friend of mine. They've got him in jail at Hahn's Peak."

"You just found out about it?"

Wayne nodded. Suddenly he wanted to enlist

this bright, gentle girl in the cause of his friend. In a few words he relayed to her what he'd just heard from Deputy Westbrook. She asked questions, and he gave quick, emphatic answers.

"Listen, Verna. Let me tell you how I got to know Jim. Couple of years ago I lost my wallet while riding a brushy range up toward Shield Mountain. Didn't miss it till I got back to the ranch. More'n a hundred dollars in it—and not one chance in a million of finding it. I'd kissed it goodbye for good when a stranger rode up and handed it to me—a cattlehand named Jim Gentry from Slater Park. He'd happened on it while looking for some Mark Lassiter strays."

"Your name was on it?"

"No—but it had a hotel receipt with my name on it. Jim Gentry could 've kept it and no one the wiser. Instead he rode forty miles to the Cary ranch and gave it to me. I offered him half the money as a reward, but he wouldn't take it. Do you think a fella like that would rob his own boss?"

"I most certainly don't," Verna agreed warmly. She turned to the man on the other side of her. "Do you know this Jim Gentry, Mr. Garrison?"

She had to repeat the question before he answered. When he did, his tone struck Brady as being strained and cautious. "Never heard of him." After a pause he added: "The law must have something on him or they wouldn't have jugged him."

The girl turned back to Wayne. "Does he have a good lawyer?"

"If he hasn't," Wayne said grimly, "I'm going to see that he gets one. Means I'll have to take a few days off and ride right through on this coach to Hahn's Peak."

"You could be a character witness," Verna suggested.

Wayne nodded, then said thoughtfully: "At district court sessions there's always a dozen lawyers on hand, from Steamboat, Hayden, Craig—even from Denver." One out-of-county lawyer, Bertram Farr from Georgetown, was sitting right in front of them now.

"My Uncle Nathan's there too," Verna reminded him. "He's a grand person, and they say he's a wonderful defense lawyer. If you like I'll give you a note of introduction."

"I already know him," Wayne said. "He's tops in Routt County. If Jim hasn't already got himself a lawyer, I'll try to line up your uncle for him."

It made a bond between them, and for the next hour they talked intimately about Jim Gentry and Attorney Nathan Bainbridge of Steamboat Springs. "The strongest evidence in the world, I've heard Uncle Nate say, is character," Verna said. "When he puts you on the stand and you tell about Jim Gentry returning your wallet, I can't imagine how any jury could convict him."

"Neither can I," Wayne agreed gratefully. "But

27

hadn't you better get a little sleep? It'll be day-light pretty soon."

Verna did sleep briefly; but Wayne Brady didn't. He sat wide-awake, thinking about Jim Gentry—and about the gentle girl near his shoulder.

Then suddenly he thought of someone else. Dale Garrison. During this last hour there'd been a strange silence from Garrison. Usually the man dominated conversations, putting himself forward, cutting in. Especially when he was trying to make time with a pretty girl.

But since the subject of a crime in Slater Park had come up, he'd spoken only once, and then only after prompting. "Never heard of him. . . . The law must have something on him or they wouldn't have jugged him."

It made a false note. In the first place, it was hardly credible that Garrison hadn't heard of Jim Gentry. Both the Steamboat Springs weeklies, and even the Denver dailies, must have headlined the Slater Park murder and robbery. Garrison could hardly have missed it. And in the second place, you don't disagree with a girl when you're trying to charm her. She'd invited a sympathetic answer, and he hadn't played up.

Why not?

III

Yampa was a swing station in Egeria Park, about halfway between Wolcott and Steamboat Springs. When the stage stopped there at sunup, a south-bound stage had just rolled in and its passengers were getting off for breakfast. The station eating house had two long tables. People from the south-bound coach took one of them and people from the northbound coach took the other.

Both coaches changed drivers at Yampa, and Brady was glad to see that George Wren was on hand to hold the ribbons from here to Steamboat Springs. Wren was reliable and always well informed. Probably he'd know the facts which had prompted Gentry's arrest.

As they filed into the eating house, Brady spoke to Walt Cody. "Look, Walt, what about changing places with me from here to the next stop? You take my seat in the coach while I ride up top with the driver."

Cody cocked a curious eye. "Thought I was doin' yuh a favor—givin' you a seat by that good-lookin', yellow-haired gal. What's the matter? Did she brush you off?"

"Not yet, Walt. I just want a little confab with George Wren. When we get to the next stop we'll trade back again."

It was settled that way, and they went on in to eat. But the delay had allowed Garrison to guide Verna to a seat at the table and take the one next to her. Mr. Milner, the Steamboat Springs banker, was on the other side of her. Wayne took the only place left, finding himself between the lawyer Farr and the Brooklyn saloon woman Mattie.

People from the other table were exchanging greetings and questions with the coachload just in from Wolcott. "When's the Moffatt line comin'?" . . . "How's everything in Omaha, Brady? Didja get a good price for those Two Circle Bar steers? . . . Hi, Luke. Did they catch the guy that shot Mark Lassiter?"

Brady noticed that Luke, at the other table, had this week's issue of the Steamboat *Pilot* in his pocket. "Mind if I borrow it a minute?"

Luke gave him the paper, and as he ate breakfast, Brady read the latest on the Slater Park sensation. Reviewing the Lassiter shooting, it gave a detail which hadn't been mentioned by Cal Westbrook: a detail so shocking that Brady couldn't forebear commenting on it to Attorney Farr at his right.

"Sneaked up to an open window and shot him in the back, it says. Takes a cold killer to do that."

"No ordinary sneak thief would do it," Farr agreed. "Certainly no run-of-the-mill ranch hand would do it. He might hang on to a wad of

30

money if it happened to drop in his lap. But it would take a pro—a hardened criminal who'd done it before—to slip up to a window and shoot a man in the back."

"May I see that paper, please?" The voice came from Brady's left, and when he turned to her he saw a look of something like panic on the face of the saloon woman Mattie.

"Sure." He handed her yesterday's copy of the *Pilot*.

A bit curiously, he watched her read the Mark Lassiter item. She gave him back the paper, then abruptly left the table with her breakfast untouched.

Brady wondered why. She could hardly be involved in the Lassiter affair herself. But she might know a background which could make her guess something—something which frightened her.

Deputy Cal Westbrook and his horse thief prisoner weren't eating at either of the long tables. They had a small table in a corner. They finished first and went back to the front seat of the coach. Other passengers finished and went out, some getting on one coach and some on the other.

When Brady himself went out, he saw that the two drivers were taking a piece of baggage off the northbound coach and strapping it to the rear of the other. Then he saw the woman Mattie getting on the Wolcott-bound stage when she should have been reboarding the one bound for Steamboat Springs.

Brady spoke to the drivers. "What made her change her mind?"

Driver George Wren gave a shrug. "Your guess is as good as mine. Said she'd just remembered she'd left something in Denver and wanted to go back for it. Paid cash for a ticket to Wolcott, and she can catch a train there."

"Doesn't make sense," Brady puzzled. "By the way, George, I'll be riding up top with you from here to the next station. Do you mind?"

"Glad to have you. Climb up, Brady. Be pulling out in a minute."

Shortly the coaches rolled away in opposite directions, Brady seated beside Wren on the one bound for Steamboat Springs and Hahn's Peak.

"You lost a passenger, George. She took a look at yesterday's *Pilot*, and something in it scared her. It was about the Lassiter killing."

"Read it myself," the driver said. "Nothing new in it."

"Nothing new to you, George, but maybe something new to Mattie. How long has she been away?"

"She headed for the Outside about a month ago," Wren remembered. "Rode my stage with a ticket to Wolcott. Asked about train connections to Denver. They come and go, those women. Likely, this one thought she could do better at one of the fancy joints on Holiday Street. Found out she couldn't, so she started back to her old stand at Brooklyn."

"Then changed her mind," Brady added, "when she read that squib about the Slater Park killing. How do you figure it, George?"

The grade here was downhill, and Wren whipped his four-in-hand to a trot. "It might make sense, Brady, if she happened to have a pretty good idea about who killed Lassiter. Might be any one of a dozen hard cases who hang around those dives at Brooklyn. As a saloon woman there, she knows all of them. One of them could have a record in another state that Mattie knows about. Maybe a killer's record that fits the way Lassiter got shot."

Wayne Brady thought it over while he rolled a cigaret. "The way Lassiter got shot, according to that paper she read, was in the back through an open window."

"Which doesn't ring true," Wren suggested, "if the killer's main purpose was to grab off Lassiter's money. A money hunter wouldn't do it that way. He'd watch for a time when nobody was there, then prowl for the money. He wouldn't start out by shooting a sneak bullet through Lassiter."

The reasoning impressed Brady. From the first he'd sensed something unconvincing about that sneak shot through an open window. "Go on, George."

"But suppose," the driver argued shrewdly, "that

33

someone had a solid reason for wanting Lassiter dead. Maybe an old grudge; or maybe some Brooklyn toughie was afraid Lassiter would identify him as a wanted outlaw from another state. So his main purpose was murder. A sneak shot from behind would do it. Once done, looking for the money could be an afterthought. He might put in as much as an hour at it before making himself scarce."

By the time Brady had weighed this theory and agreed with it, the stage was rattling down Watson Creek. A piny forest enclosed them on both sides.

"Let's get back to Mattie, George. Did Lassiter ever go over to Brooklyn, on his trips to Steamboat?"

"Yes—but only for a beer or two on a hot day. Almost any man in Steamboat 'll take a walk across the bridge now and then, Steamboat being bone dry. If he's a married man he'll likely do it at night; if he's single he'll do it in broad daylight. Mark Lassiter was a bachelor and fairly straightlaced. All he'd want over there would be a cold beer on a hot day; and then only when he was on some errand to Steamboat Springs."

"Which saloon did Mattie hang out in?"

"All of them. Three saloons and a bawdy over there. The bawdy women circulate from bar to bar. Let's say Mattie read about the Slater Park killing in a Denver paper. She half suspects one of those Brooklyn rowdies because of his past record. But not till she gets to Yampa does she learn the exact method—a sneak shot in the back through an open window. It scares her. What happened to Lassiter could happen to anyone else who knows about the killer's past. So she turns around and heads back for the Outside."

To Steamboat Springs people, anywhere east of the range was called the Outside.

Brady said: "The police have a name for it, don't they—some foreign word?"

"*Modus operandi,*" George Wren supplied. Having once served a term as town marshal at Steamboat Springs, he'd seen circulars using the term in connection with wanted men.

They stopped at a wayside store called Phippsburg and took on a mail sack. The trail beyond led along the clear riffles of the Yampa River near its headwaters. Wren alternately walked and trotted his team.

"You'll be getting off at Steamboat, Brady?"

"I'd planned to. But now I'll ride right through to the Peak. Want to see if I can help Jim Gentry. Just what does the sheriff think he's got on Jim?"

"Nothing but opportunity, far as I know. They say he was the only one there after the killer left. So he was the only one who could have read the note and used it to locate the money. A bit of politics in it too, maybe."

"What politics?" Brady questioned.

35

"Folks 've been riding Sheriff Farnham for not cleaning out a nest of outlaws in Brown's Park, in the west end of the county. The two Steamboat weeklies are feuding about it. The *Sentinel* backs Farnham; but the *Pilot* claims he's soft on those outlaws. They claim he looks the other way whenever any devilment goes on over there. It's likely to lick Farnham at the next election. So to mend his fences, maybe he cracked down on the only suspect he could turn up in the Lassiter case: your friend Gentry."

At the next stage station, Yellowjacket, while they were changing horses, Wayne Brady again traded places with Walt Cody. By then Dale Garrison was his old talkative self and was confidently promoting himself with Verna Bainbridge. He'd just finished dating her for supper tonight when Brady joined them.

Would mention of the Slater Park case quiet him down again? Brady tried it, but this time Garrison himself joined in.

"Sounds like a couple of smart hunches," he agreed promptly when Brady outlined the two ideas suggested by George Wren. "I wondered why she quit us." He nodded toward the front seat, which was now occupied only by a deputy and his prisoner. "She could be afraid that what happened to Lassiter could happen to her. So she ducks out. And that hunch about why the killer went there sounds reasonable. Looking for money only an afterthought, huh?"

"You'll report this to the sheriff at Steamboat?" Verna asked Brady.

Garrison beat Brady to the answer. "Sheriff 'll be attending court at Hahn's Peak, likely. But he's got an undersheriff at Steamboat and George Wren's a cinch to tip him off. Undersheriff Jack Camp. Jack'll go over to Brooklyn and give those rowdies a close look. Shake 'em down and find out if any of 'em has a past connection with Mattie."

They were out of the timber now and in a broad valley of hay meadows, although still under the shadow of high, piny mountains. Off to the right the forest sloped steeply up to Rabbit Ears' Pass. At the crossing of Priest Creek a rancher flagged the stage down, and Wren stopped to let him ride into town.

As midday approached, the valley widened, and just at noon they struck the east end of Steamboat Springs' main street, where Wren whipped to a run. He always liked to arrive with a flourish. Looking out a left coach window, Brady could see the riffling Yampa River lined with dark green cottonwoods, and through them he could see a row of saloons on the far bank. A bridge gave to them at the foot of Fifth Street. Big John's place on the right; then Bart Tarkio's; then the Yampa Roundup run by Jeffry Silverton. Beyond them he could see a shuttered two-storey frame known as Bonnie's Place. Each of the four houses had a hitchrack. A few saddle mounts stood cock-kneed at the saloon racks; but Bonnie's hitchrail at this noonday hour was empty.

Brooklyn, they called that vice nest, and Brady had only a glimpse of it while the stagecoach flashed by. Beyond Seventh there were board sidewalks and stores. The walks had shoppers and idlers; the hitchrails had wagons and riding horses. They rolled by three general merchandise stores—Duffield's, Adair's and Abner Barnett's. Barnett's, in a wide, two-storey brick, was the biggest of them all.

The next block had a livery barn, two restaurants, and a smithy; then the Hugus Building with a bank on the ground floor and Hugus Hall upstairs. A sign over the Hugus Hall windows said that *Kathleen Mavourneen* would be playing tonight, with local talent. Brady saw Doctor Clark Wingo and Town Marshal Burgess on the walk in front of Barry's Billiard Hall; then the Wintersteen Building and Doctor Neuman's drugstore. A pair of burros scampered out of the way as George Wren galloped his team by them. With a rasp of brakes he drew up in front of the Sheridan Hotel.

"Eating stop!" he shouted. "In thirty minutes we'll be leaving for Hahn's Peak."

As passengers climbed out and filed into the

hotel, Brady reluctantly abandoned Verna to Dale Garrison in order to get in a few words with Undersheriff Jack Camp. Camp had just come out of the *Pilot* office across the street and was headed toward the hotel. Wren, after turning his coach over to Bill Marshman, who would drive it to Hahn's Peak, was waiting by Brady when Camp joined them.

The undersheriff listened alertly while Wren told about Mattie leaving the stage at Yampa and his ideas about why she'd done so. Then he let loose a bombshell of his own.

"I've another good reason," he told them, "for thinking that Lassiter was shot by someone from Brooklyn. You know Old Man Yancy?"

Both Wren and Brady nodded. Yancy was an old-time prospector who'd spent the last thirty years packing rock around the north end of Routt County.

"He only comes to town whenever he needs a grub pack. Came in yesterday after camping a month up by Saddle Mountain. Know where that is?"

Again both men nodded. Saddle Mountain was only about a mile southwest of Slater Park.

"Last night he crossed the bridge for a few drinks at Brooklyn. Took one at each bar, hoping he might run into one of his old Hahn's Peak buddies. Yancy was one of the original gold-rushers who came in with Joe Hahn and Captain

Way, back in '66. Along about midnight Yancy crossed back over the bridge to Lincoln Street and went to the jail. Told the night jailor he wanted to see me. The jailor said I was at home in bed, but if it was important he'd get a message to me. 'Tell him,' Old Man Yancy said, 'that I've been in camp a month and have just heard about Mark Lassiter gettin' shot. They say it happened on a Tuesday morning three weeks ago. That was the morning I was out stalking a deer for camp meat. Just as I was crossing the Beef Trail, a little this side of Slater Park, a man on a horse almost ran over me. I got a good look at him; don't know whether he saw me or not. He was heading south out of Slater Park at a hard run. Next time I saw him was tonight, at a bar over in Brooklyn.'

" 'His name?' the jailor asked. But Yancy didn't know the man's name, only his face. 'Tell Jack Camp to meet me over there in half an hour and I'll point him out.'

"Then Yancy left to go back to Brooklyn. The jailor lost a little time finding someone to watch the jail; we don't allow him to leave his prisoners unguarded. He had to walk to my house on Oak Street to wake me up. After that I had to dress, saddle a horse, and ride to Brooklyn. When I got there Yancy wasn't at any of the three saloons; nor at Bonnie's Place, either. Bartenders and customers remembered seeing him over there before midnight. They said he left but never

40

came back. I figured it was a false alarm and came home.

"An hour after daylight we found Yancy. He lay face up in the riffles of the Yampa River, just under the Fifth Street bridge, with his head bashed in. Only one way it could have happened."

Wren nodded. "Only one way, Jack. When Yancy left the saloons, the killer followed him and saw him go into the Steamboat Springs jail. We know he's an open window sneak. So he likely heard Yancy arrange to meet a lawman at Brooklyn and point a finger. So the killer went back to the bridge and laid for him."

"In the dark," the undersheriff added grimly. "When Yancy headed back toward Saloon Row he never got any farther than the bridge."

The ruthlessness of it sickened Brady. He went into the Sheridan Hotel to eat, but chose a seat well apart from Verna Bainbridge. She'd ask questions; and the answers were too ugly for a young girl just in from Ohio.

IV

When the coach pulled out for Hahn's Peak, it had four new passengers to replace Walt Cody, Verna Bainbridge, Dale Garrison, and the woman who'd left it at Yampa. County Clerk Withers was riding home to the Peak after a day in Steamboat. The other new passengers were shaggy, hard-rock miners.

Again Wayne Brady rode up top with the driver, who was now Bill Marshman. "How come you didn't change to the Craig stage?" Marshman asked him. "You still work for the Carys, don'tcha?"

"I just mailed them a note," Wayne explained, "saying I need to take a few days off. Want to show up in court at the Peak and try to help Jim Gentry."

"You'll have a heck of a time findin' a place to sleep," the driver warned him. "They're stacked up three in a room at Mrs. Larson's hotel. Must be forty–fifty people camped in tents all around town. Always that way at district court sessions. Lawyers, witnesses, jurymen. Rest of the year the town's dang near empty; gettin' more and more like a ghost town allatime. Wonder why they don't move the county seat to Steamboat or Hayden or Craig."

"They will, some day," Brady predicted. After making himself a cigaret he added: "Did you notice Big John sitting in a rig right across the street when the stage pulled in? Like he was waiting for someone. Mattie, likely. No way he could have known about her getting off at Yampa."

"Could be," Marshman said. "Or maybe he was waiting to see if Otto Bundchu came in on the stage. Two or three people been watchin' out for Otto. Betcha we'll find a couple more of 'em meetin' us at Hahn's Peak, to see if Otto gets off."

The name was new to Brady. "Who's Otto Bundchu?"

"He's been in the state pen at Canon City for the last ten years. His term was up Monday. If he comes straight to Routt County, like everyone expects him to, he could be on this stage right now."

"What did he do, Bill? Rob a bank?"

"He was convicted of killing Karl Janvers. Claimed self defense, and nobody could be sure it wasn't; so they only gave him twelve years. He gets out in ten and is a cinch to head right back to Hahn's Peak."

"Fill me in, Bill. I wasn't around here ten years ago."

"Karl Janvers was a Hahn's Peak prospector. A loner. Always went out by himself. Took along nothing but a horse and a pack mare, a camp kit and a grub pack. No one ever knew where he went. It's only a three-months season up there in the high country. Deep snow the other nine months. So he'd go out in mid-June and come back in mid-September.

"For three straight years he came back to Hahn's Peak with a quart can full of gold dust and nuggets. Never did file a claim. To keep people from tagging along after him each fall, he said it was just a small pocket that had played out on him. They believed him the first year. But when he showed up at the end of the next summer with another quart can full of gold, they didn't. When he went out the next June after that, half a dozen miners tried to follow him. But he saw them coming and led them the wrong way. Finally he ditched them in the middle of a rainy night and they never saw him again till late September, when for the third time he trailed into Hahn's Peak with a quart of gold."

Brady gave a low whistle. "What did he do with it? Three quarts of gold would add up to a big stake. Let's see: a quart of water weighs two pounds, and they told me in school that the specific gravity of gold is nineteen. Makes thirty-eight pounds for one quart of gold. At eighteen dollars an ounce, three quarts would be worth about twenty-five thousand dollars."

"That's just about what a Steamboat Springs bank gave him for it," Marshman remembered. "Janvers always wintered in Steamboat, where he kept a room; when he died he had thirty thousand dollars in the bank."

"Did he ever go out again after those three big summers?"

"The fourth summer, he went out but he didn't come back. Again several people tried to tag along from Hahn's Peak and again he led them in a circle and finally ditched them. All but one. Otto

44

Bundchu managed to pick up his tracks and follow him to we don't know where. He watched from the woods and saw Janvers start panning gold. We don't know what creek or gulch it was. Some think it was up around Whisky Park; some figure it was east of here near the Continental Divide; others think it was across the state line in Wyoming."

"Otto Bundchu shot him to jump the gulch?"

"That was the jury's verdict," Bill Marshman said. "When Bundchu walked in on Janvers there was a shootout—maybe an even break like Bundchu claims, or maybe a cold-blood killing. Otto won't tell where it happened; he's the only one in the world who can go back there—which he figures to do when he gets out of prison. He figures he can make himself rich. A bar rich enough to yield one panner about three thousand dollars a month for nine months oughta be worth going back to."

"How and where did they catch Bundchu?"

"Otto didn't want Janvers' body found there—because it would be a tip-off to someone else. So he loaded everything on Janvers' horse and pack mare and led them many miles away. We don't know in what direction. The body was found under a brushpile on Middle Fork of the Little Snake. The horse and pack mare were found grazing just east of Shield Mountain. Janvers' saddle and camp outfit were never found.

45

Bundchu would have gotten clean away, except he was greedy enough to keep Janvers' watch and wallet. They were on him when he was picked up and searched. The law was looking for him because he was one of those known to have followed Janvers out of Hahn's Peak."

"So he's been in prison for ten years."

Marshman nodded. "He was set free four or five days ago and any stage from the Outside could bring him to Routt County."

They came to Big Creek, and the driver walked his team across the timber bridge there. To the east a forest-land rose abruptly toward Horse Thief Peak, while to the West the range was open except for tree lines along the streams. A buckboard from Columbine drew aside to let them pass. Further on they met a load of lumber heading for Steamboat Springs from the Sand Mountain sawmill.

Brady asked: "What's all this got to do with Big John? I mean the Brooklyn saloonman who met this stage at noon. You said maybe he was expecting Otto Bundchu to be on it."

"A fair bet he was, Brady. Ten years ago, in 1891, Big John ran a saloon at Hahn's Peak. His customers were miners and prospectors and they'd sometimes cash their dust and nuggets at his bar. Big John never did any mining himself. But now and then he'd grubstake a prospector for a share in any claim he staked. One of his customers was Otto Bundchu."

"He grubstaked Bundchu?"

"No. But when Bundchu was tried for the murder of Janvers, Big John made a deal with him. He offered to finance the defense—bring in a topnotch lawyer from Denver—and if he got Otto acquitted, Otto agreed to tell Big John where the Janvers gold bar was so that Big John could send a few of his friends there to file on it."

Brady mulled it over a minute. "But Otto wasn't acquitted; so now he doesn't owe Big John a thing."

"That's right; but Big John isn't likely to figure it that way. He put a wad of dough into Otto's defense, and if he hadn't, chances are Otto would've been hanged. So he figures Otto still oughta tip him to Janvers' gold bar. Anyway he's been meeting every stage from the Outside."

"And if Otto holds out on him?"

"He might wind up like Yancy; at the bottom of a river. Big John wouldn't do it himself; but he's got a tough crew of heelers over there in Brooklyn. My guess is he'll say to Otto: 'Look, Otto; you dassent go back yourself to that pay gravel; if you do you'll be followed by a dozen men at Hahn's Peak who're laying for you there right now. They'd stake out that gulch and beat you to the courthouse with the filings. So if you're smart you'll let me handle it. Tell me where the place is and I'll send three or four men there; men who won't be followed. They can

47

file a claim for you and another for me, then help themselves to the rest.' "

The stagecoach had turned up Elk River with big willow-leaf cottonwoods lining its banks. A mile or so later, they pulled up at the Moon Hill relay station where fresh horses were traced on. Not till they were rolling again did Brady bring up his own errand—to help win an acquittal for Jim Gentry.

"Which reminds me," Bill Marshman cut in shrewdly, "of an odd overlap between the killing of Janvers and the killing of Mark Lassiter."

Wayne Brady gave a puzzled stare. "There can't be," he protested. "You say Janvers was killed ten years ago—long before Lassiter came to Colorado."

"Just the same, there's a connection," the driver insisted. "Remember I said when Janvers died he had thirty thousand dollars in a Steamboat Springs bank. He was a single man and left no will. No blood kin that anyone knew about. It looked like his money would have to be assigned to the state—when someone took another look at the wallet they'd found on Bundchu. A wallet swiped from Janvers. A scrap of paper there had an address on it. No name; just a ranch near Tucson, Arizona. They wrote to that ranch and found out that its foreman was Mark Lassiter; and Lassiter turned out to be the son of Janvers' sister, no longer living; which made Lassiter a blood kin nephew. So in the end the Steamboat Springs bank account went to Lassiter at Tucson. He put it in a Tucson bank which went bust in the money panic of 1893. It left Lassiter without a cent except what he had in his pockets. Made him bitter against banks; said he'd never trust one of them again. And he never did. To get a fresh start he decided to move to Routt County, Colorado, where friends of his late uncle might give him a job. Ended up by filing a homestead in Slater Park, which in eight years he built into a first class little ranch."

It explained Lassiter's distrust of banks and why he hadn't banked his steer-sale money. It might, Brady brooded, explain something else too. Since Lassiter had come here from Arizona, maybe the saloon woman, Mattie, or Big John, or Jeffry Silverton, or some other Brooklyn hard case had also come here from Arizona. Maybe some desert killer with a record of having shot a man through an open window.

Had someone like that been spotted by Mark Lassiter?

They stopped at the Clark post office only long enough to drop off a mail bag. There the stage road left the Elk River and followed northerly up Willow Creek. Timbered mountains were closing in on both sides, and the air had a high country tang. To the west the sun dipped toward the crests of the Elkheads. Slater Park lay over that way.

Late in the afternoon, they sighted the tall, magically perfect cone of Hahn's Peak almost directly ahead. A county seat of that name lay in a gulch at the near foot of it, and tomorrow Jim Gentry would go on trial there. With no recent mineral strikes of importance, and snowed-in more than half of each year, the place might have become a ghost town except for the spring and fall sessions of the Routt County district court.

"Poverty Bar, the miners call it," Marshman said. "Look at those campers."

They were wheeling into the single rutty street, and Brady could see tents and supper fires along a gulch to the left of it. Litigants, jurors, witnesses for whom there'd be no room at the one small hotel—they'd be gone in a few days, leaving nothing but a little frame courthouse, jail, stage barn, saloon, the Withers store, and the Larson Hotel, plus a row of shabby cabins. Even most of these would be deserted when the deep snows came.

Right now the street had people: rawboned miners in from Way's Gulch and other nearby camps where gold-seekers were still stubbornly panning; a score of bearded men standing on the hotel walk when Marshman drew up there; and a few lawyers waiting for expected witnesses. County Sheriff Farnham was there to see if his deputy would arrive with a horse-thief prisoner. Miners, saloon idlers. Mrs. Larson herself was there, and she smiled regretfully at the first passenger who disembarked. "Sorry. We're full up."

Marshman's gaze fixed on a weatherbeaten prospector who was alertly eyeing each disembarking passenger. He nudged Brady. "See that skinny red-neck? Ten years ago he tagged along after Karl Janvers the last time Karl left here." The driver chuckled and raised his voice. "Otto didn't show up today, Skinny. Try again tomorrow."

When the coach was empty, Marshman whipped his team on to the stage barn and unhitched there. Beyond lay only wilderness. This was the high, lonely end of the Wolcott, Steamboat Springs, and Hahn's Peak run.

V

It took Wayne Brady only a few minutes to find out that there wasn't an empty cot in town. "They're sleeping on the barroom floor," he was told.

He went to the little log jail expecting to find Jim Gentry in a cell there. But the jail had only one prisoner—the horse thief who'd arrived on today's stage. The man stared sullenly at Brady through the cell bars—the same cell, Brady remembered, which three years ago had housed the two most deadly outlaws in the history of northwest Colorado: a pair who'd killed often and wantonly in three states. Sheriff Nieman's posse had captured them in Brown's Park after a gun battle in which one deputy and one outlaw had been shot dead. The leaders, Harry Tracy and Dave Lant, had been captured alive and taken ninety miles over midwinter snows to this Hahn's Peak jail—only to escape at night by tricking Sheriff Nieman into their cell and batting him down. With his keys and his gun they'd slipped through darkness to the stage barn where they'd helped themselves to a pair of stage horses. The sheriff, coming slowly to his senses, had chased them forty miles through sub-zero cold, recapturing them on the Yampa River.

Now there was another sheriff, Farnham, and here in the same cell was another prisoner, a run-of-the-mill horse thief not to be compared with those notorious killers, Tracy and Lant.

"What about Jim Gentry?" Wayne asked the jailor.

"He posted bail." The jailor was a small, bald man with the ivory butt of a six-gun showing at his belt. "They say he's camped in the woods somewhere, waitin' for court tomorrow."

Wayne nodded. Bail would be admissible, since there was no murder charge involved. "Know if he has a lawyer?"

"Tom Gorman of Craig, I've heard."

Wayne found Gorman eating supper at the

Larson Hotel. He squeezed into a seat beside the lawyer at the table there. "Maybe you can use me as a character witness," he suggested. "I'm a friend of Jim Gentry."

"I sure can, young fella. How long have you known my client?"

Wayne told about Jim Gentry returning a lost wallet, then said, "Glad to know he's got a good lawyer. If he didn't have one I figured on trying to line up Nate Bainbridge of Steamboat Springs. I rode a stage from Wolcott with his niece."

Gorman thought it over a minute. "Look, Brady; I've been associated with Bainbridge a couple of times. He's a genius at handling human interest witnesses. If you like, I'll invite him to be co-counsel and let him put you on the stand."

"Thanks, Mr. Gorman. See you in court tomorrow."

Now, hours later, Wayne Brady was bedded down in the stage stable hay loft. It was better than sleeping out-of-doors without a bedroll. Under and around him was prairie hay with a sweet meadow smell to it. He was far enough away from saloon noise to allow a quiet sleep. The long ride from Wolcott had left him bone-weary. Still for a while he lay wakeful, thinking of tomorrow's court trial and of a pretty girl who'd ridden a coach with him over the range. He'd look her up again, soon as Jim was out of trouble.

A mule brayed down the street, and a crowd of miners passed, camp-bound after an evening at the Hahn's Peak bar. Then quiet again except for the champing of stage horses in stalls below this loft.

For a while longer Wayne lay wakeful, here in a hay loft at Hahn's Peak. Many times Routt County old-timers had told him about the rugged and cruelly tragic history of this camp. How three men, Joseph Hahn, William Doyle, and Captain George Way had come here in 1865 and found gold in a gulch at the foot of the towering cone they named Hahn's Peak. How they'd returned a year later with a party of fifty men to name and prospect six gulches—Hahn's Gulch, Way's Gulch, Doyle's Gulch, and three others. How in the fall deep snows had driven them all out except Hahn, Way, and Doyle.

The three had tried to winter here, but deep snows drove all the game out of the region. No deer, no elk, no rabbits, no birds. The bitter edge of starvation had forced them to try to make it over the divide on snowshoes—with Hahn and Way perishing on the trail and with only Doyle finally getting out, snowblind.

Two summers later, some of their friends had drifted back to build cabins and found a camp which they called Hahn's Peak. Because it was the only settlement in Routt County, it had to be the county seat and, by some miracle, still was. Much gold had been taken from the six gulches, but after a few years it had begun playing out. Snowbound and almost deserted in winters, in summers it still attracted gold-seekers who kept stubbornly at it all the way from Whisky Park to Elk River. It made enough trade to support a saloon and a store at Hahn's Peak.

The only real importance of the place, now, came at sessions of the district court. Some day even that would be gone, when common sense made them move the county seat to Steamboat Springs.

It was Brady's last thought before he fell asleep.

Some time during the night a sound wakened him. It came from the barn aisle directly below this loft. In a moment he heard it again—the rebellious snort of a horse followed by a muttered oath. Next Brady was aware of a faint, brief flare of light. It shone upward from an open trap in the loft floor—an opening through which hay could be forked down into a stall manger.

His guess was that someone had struck a match while groping in darkness down there. A regular hostler wouldn't do that. If he had an errand in the barn, he'd come with a lighted lantern. Only a prowler would grope in the dark.

Again a snort, and then hoof sounds on the floor boards of a stall. Someone, Brady decided, was in the act of stealing a horse.

He heard the horse being led forward to the barn vestibule. Then a minute of stillness followed by a thump. Brady remembered seeing a saddle draped over a saddle tree in the barn vestibule. Probably the thief was now saddling the horse. It had to be a thief, because an honest man would have brought a lantern.

At the front of the loft was an open hay door through which wagonloads of hay could be pitchforked up here. Starlight limned it as a dim rectangle of grayness for Brady. He crawled to it over the hay and peered down just in time to see a man lead a saddled horse from the barn.

It was too dark for him to recognize a face; but he made out a white gun butt sticking from the man's belt. A gun with an ivory or white bone grip! Only a few hours ago Brady had seen such a gun. The armed jailor had worn it; an ivory-handled six-gun.

Now another man wore it, and was slipping out of this barn with a stolen horse. There could only be one answer. History was repeating itself. The escape of Tracy and Lant, three years ago, was being reenacted by this horse thief. Like Tracy and Lant, by some trick he'd lured a jailor to the cell and knocked him out. Like Tracy and Lant, after taking the jailor's gun, keys, and matches, he'd stolen an escape mount from the stage barn.

Directly below the loft door the man put a foot into a stirrup and swung to the saddle. In another minute he'd be gone, and by morning would have a long headstart through the forest. Unarmed himself, Wayne Brady had only one way to stop him. He made a flying leap from the hay loft door and landed astride the mounted man's back.

The horse reared—and the two men hit hard-packed ground. The jar threw them apart, and each man scrambled to his feet, the armed man whipping out an ivory-butted gun. The shot came just as Brady dove headfirst at his stomach, and again both men went down, Brady grappling the other's middle. The man kicked at him, punched, clawed; pain stabbed Brady's ankle as a kick raked it, then he tasted blood at his mouth as a solid punch hit there. The horse was still snorting, plunging. The two men rolled on the ground with Brady holding his clinch, the other man clawing with his left hand while his right reached for the gun which had been jarred from it.

Men from the saloon came running. A lantern flickered in the dark. The gunshot had been heard and was drawing people this way.

One of the first to arrive was Sheriff Farnham. A glance identified the man who should be in a jail cell. The jailor's gun and a saddled horse gave the rest of the story.

Farnham helped Brady to his feet. "Thanks, cowboy. If he'd got away my name would be Mud at the next election. Somebody go see what happened at the jail. Then fetch a doctor to patch this boy up."

The patches were in place, over cuts and bruises

on lip, chin, and cheek, when Wayne Brady appeared in the courtroom at ten in the morning. When he was called to the witness stand by co-counsel for the defense Nathan Bainbridge, he walked with a limp. An ankle bruise from a vicious kick still pained him.

The story was all over camp now. Each of the twelve jurors had heard it—and the effect was to make a hero out of a cowboy who'd just saved the county authorities from a humiliating disgrace. A repetition of the Tracy–Lant escape would have been hard to live down. It presented an opportunity which Nathan Bainbridge made the most of.

"Unable to find other accommodations, Mr. Brady, you bedded down in the stage barn hay loft last night?"

"Yes."

"You were asleep when sounds from below wakened you?"

"Yes."

"Describe what happened." Attorney Bainbridge was a tall, lean man with wiry black hair and bony, Lincolnesque features.

Brady told of jumping from the loft to grapple with a mounted thief.

"The man was armed?"

"Yes, with the jailor's gun."

"And you were unarmed?"

"Yes."

"He fired at you point-blank?"

"Yes."

"Yet nevertheless you clinched with him, holding him till authorities arrived?"

"Yes." The patches on Brady's face confirmed him. Bainbridge gazed at them a moment, giving jurymen time to do the same.

"You know the defendant, James Gentry?"

"Yes."

"Under what circumstances did you meet him?"

Brady told about the return of a lost wallet.

"In your opinion, is the defendant a man of exceptional integrity?"

"He is."

"That is all."

There was no cross-examination. District Attorney Gray was anxious to get this hero-of-the-hour out of the jury's sight.

Lawyer Tom Gorman, in his summation plea, said: "The state has presented no case except an assertion that the defendant was the only person who had an opportunity to dig up Lassiter's money. Yet one to five hours elapsed between the murder and the theft. During that time, some other and unknown man might have come by, read the note, and by it been directed to the money cache. This possibility creates more than a reasonable doubt as to the defendant's guilt. On that ground, and on the record of his past integrity, the defense pleads for acquittal."

The jury was out only a few minutes. Its verdict was not guilty.

A free man, Jim Gentry gratefully took Brady to the saloon to celebrate with a drink. "You saved my bacon, Pardner. Puttin' on that scrap at the barn and tellin' what a good guy I am."

"Where'll you go from here, Jim?"

"To a job at the U Bar. That's where I was the day Lassiter was killed; to line up a job after he sold his land. The U Bar said okay, they'd be glad to take me on whenever Mark didn't need me any more."

Half a dozen men who'd heard the verdict drifted in. Several of them slapped Brady on the back, hailing him for his midnight leap on an escaping jailbird. Toward Jim Gentry they were markedly less cordial. It struck Brady that some of them had their fingers crossed as to Jim's innocence. A jury had acquitted him, but . . .

A big ruddy man wearing a cowman's hat and boots came in. Brady had spotted him in the courtroom and knew him as Ben Sallisaw, owner of the U Bar on lower Slater Creek.

Jim Gentry's face lighted up. "There comes my new boss." He advanced to meet the man. "Hi, Mr. Sallisaw. I'm ready to go to work now. When do you want me to show up?"

Sallisaw looked at him, and Brady saw a shadow of uncertainty on his face. Almost at once he sensed what was coming.

"I won't be needing you after all, Gentry," the man said. "Took on a couple of hands from Baggs the other day and they fill me out."

The U Bar man turned to the bar and ordered whisky. Wayne Brady looked at shock on Jim's face, and his own felt a flush of resentment. If it was that way with Sallisaw, there'd always be a slight, nagging doubt as to Jim's innocence. As long as there was only one chance in a hundred that Jim Gentry had robbed an employer, no other cattleman was likely to take him on.

As Brady went out with his friend, both of them knew that only one thing could completely vindicate Jim. "I gotta find out who really did it," Jim concluded bitterly. "Somebody came by there after Mark was dead. He read the note and took the money."

"Till we run him down," Brady agreed, "you'll be getting the Ben Sallisaw treatment all over the county."

"We?"

"Yes. We." Somehow Brady found himself militantly and angrily involved in his friend's predicament. "I'm siding you to the finish, Jim. We'll need to stop cowboying for a while and start being range detectives. Right now I've got to go to Hayden and report to the Cary brothers. They owe me some time off. Two or three weeks ought to do it. Meet me in Steamboat three days from now and we'll start from there."

61

VI

A noon later, the stagecoach from Wolcott brought Otto Bundchu to Steamboat Springs. A dozen people on the lookout for him included the editors of both the *Pilot* and the *Sentinel*. Big John from Brooklyn was there, as well as a pair of alert gold-seekers from Hahn's Peak. Others who were merely curious stood on the Sheridan Hotel walk. Both the weeklies had speculated as to the likelihood of Otto coming directly here from prison. Otherwise they might not have recognized him. His face had a prison pallor, and he was twenty pounds lighter than he'd been ten years ago.

The newsmen got to him first. "It's only a thirty minute stop here," the *Pilot* man reminded him. "Just time for a quick statement. You're heading for the Peak, I take it?"

"My ticket," Otto told him, "reads only to Steamboat." He took his bag from the stage and handed it to the hotel porter.

"You'll lay over here a day and go on up tomorrow?" the *Sentinel* man prompted.

"Nope." The ex-convict's response was emphatic. "For me this is the end of the line. You can put me up, Mr. Monson?"

Harry Monson, proprietor of the Sheridan,

could only nod. He had many vacant rooms and everyone knew it.

By this time Big John had left his buggy and crossed the street. He clapped Otto on the shoulder. "Why don't you come over and stay with me, Otto? You remember me, don'tcha? John Nolan. Had a bar up at the Peak in the old days. I put up the dough for your defense, remember?"

Bundchu remembered, but declined the offer. "Rather stay over here, John. Nearer the bath house. I'm sort of run down, and maybe those sulphur baths 'll pick me up."

Steamboat Springs had taken its name from a cluster of mammoth mineral springs which gushed from rocks along the Yampa River almost directly across from this hotel.

An old-timer from Hahn's Peak edged in. "But what about the Karl Janvers gold gulch, Otto? You'll be stakin' a claim there, won'tcha?"

Bundchu made a grimace and shook his head. "Nope. My mining days are over. Anyway, I couldn't find that place after all this time." He brushed through the sidewalk crowd and followed the coach passengers into the lobby. There he registered and was assigned a second floor room.

He went directly up to it and didn't come down until the stage passengers had finished eating and the stage had pulled out for Hahn's Peak. In the lobby he was again waylaid, and again he brushed everyone off. "To hell with mining! All it ever got me was trouble. If there's any gold left up there you boys can have it."

No one believed him. Everyone was sure that it was just a ruse to keep men from trailing along when he set out for the Janvers gold gulch.

In the dining room, stagecoach passengers had been replaced by local people and regular hotel guests. Business men and store clerks were at a long center table. At a small table by the wall a pretty young woman with flaxen hair was lunching with a man who didn't look like a native westerner. The waitress, not sure that people would want to sit with an ex-convict, gave Bundchu a table by himself.

Otto didn't mind. The more he was left to himself, the better he'd like it. He didn't intend to stay here more than a week. During that time he'd actually make use of the mineral baths in order to excuse his presence here. On the main point he'd told the truth: he had no intention of going on to Hahn's Peak—least of all to a mystery bonanza where ten years ago he'd killed Karl Janvers.

For that decision he had three solid reasons. First, prison and an additional ten years of age had softened him physically, so that he no longer had the rugged stamina required to wash out gold in a wilderness gulch. Second, Karl Janvers had been more than commonly popular around Hahn's

Peak, and one of Karl's old friends up there might want to avenge his murder. A rough, tough bunch, those old-timers, and Otto was determined to get no closer to them than he was right now.

Third, at the very least some of them would be sure to follow him to the Janvers pay gravel. To go there Otto would need to outfit himself with a mule or burro and a camp kit. If he should leave Hahn's Peak equipped like that, everyone would know where he was going. They'd gang up on him and stake the gulch for themselves.

Otto had a much safer plan—one to which he'd given much thought in the long tedious hours of his prison life. To put it over he'd need the help of a man named Ambrose Kincaid.

He'd never seen Kincaid in his life; nor had Kincaid ever seen him. But he knew that Kincaid was a broker in mining properties with an office in Steamboat Springs.

Maybe Kincaid was one of those men at the long center table. Otto listened to their talk. He heard one of them addressed as Mr. Milner; another as Mr. Duffield. Another seemed to be a druggist named Killon. The man they called Burgess had a badge which identified him as the town marshal. The tall, quiet man seemed to be a United States Land Commissioner named Wintersteen.

No Kincaid. What about the man eating with the pretty young girl? Otto heard her call him Mr.

Garrison, while the man himself was calling the girl Verna. So he wasn't Kincaid. It was clear to Otto that the man was doing his best to promote himself romantically.

Later Otto bought the current issue of the Steamboat *Pilot* and sat in the lobby reading it. The leftmost front page column began with a roster of county officers; underneath this, in neat boxes, were a number of professional cards. Three doctors, four lawyers, a building contractor, and then a mining consultant. The mining man's card said:

AMBROSE KINCAID
MINES AND MINING STOCK
APPRAISALS—CONSULTATIONS
Office over Killon's drugstore—7th & Lincoln
Residence, the Onyx Hotel—7th & Oak

Presently Otto took a walk down Lincoln Avenue to the Seventh Street corner. Killon's drugstore there had office rooms above it, and a front upper window had Ambrose Kincaid's name. The window was open, and beyond it a man seated at a desk was sure to be Kincaid. He had a short Van Dyke beard and the look of a successful professional man. Bundchu studied his profile for a few minutes, dubiously. According to a fellow inmate of the Canon City penitentiary, Ambrose Kincaid had a criminal past. Was it true?

In a little while Otto walked a block north to 7th & Oak. A rambling frame building there had the name ONYX HOTEL on it. Being only a block from his office, it made a convenient place for Kincaid to live.

What were his habits? What was his standing here in Routt County? Otto decided to find out before making an approach.

Walking back up Lincoln to the Sheridan, he saw that the street hadn't changed much since he'd left here ten years ago. The only new business block of importance seemed to be a two-storey brick building housing the Abner Barnett General Merchandise store. The name was new to Otto. The store was bristling with trade, shoppers moving in and out, ranch wagons hitched in front.

Back in the Sheridan lobby Bundchu took today's *Pilot* from his pocket and read every local item in it, including the advertizements. The biggest display ad was for Abner Barnett's store. A news item reported progress at the Turner mine on Little Red Park Creek, above Hahn's Peak, claiming that the ore would assay better than one hundred dollars per ton. Two recent murders were reviewed, both unsolved. A rancher named Lassiter had been shot dead in Slater Park; a veteran prospector named Yancy had been slugged and dumped into the Yampa River from the bridge which crossed to Brooklyn. There was a definite link, the paper said, between the two crimes, and

67

suspicion pointed toward some unknown habitue of the vice suburb across the river.

Otto tossed the paper aside. He remembered Yancy, but he'd never heard of Lassiter. His concern now was to inform himself as to the habits and local standing of Ambrose Kincaid.

As he idled in the lobby, several times he was approached and asked if he wouldn't be going up to Hahn's Peak in a few days. Always he gave the same answer. No; he was through with mining. He'd skinned his knuckles on a sluice trough for the last time.

He didn't want to bring up the subject of Ambrose Kincaid, but late in the afternoon the name was brought up by someone else. An ex–stage driver, Walt Cody, took a seat by him and stoked a short-stemmed pipe. Otto vaguely remembered him as a friendly chap, talkative, and probably as well informed as anyone else about the Who's Who of Routt County.

"You've kinda left us holdin' the bag, Otto," Walt chuckled. "Folks 've been waitin' fer you to show up so you could lead 'em to Janvers' gulch. Now you say you're not goin' back there at all."

"You heard right," Otto confirmed. "If you ask me, that Hahn's Peak country is a snare and a delusion."

"Mebbeso," Walt conceded. "But it won't be after the Moffatt line gets here. They's some mines up there that 'd pay big if it wasn't fer the long haul to a railroad. Take the *Tom Thum* on the slope of Hahn's Peak; or the *Minnie D* up around Columbine; or the *Elkhorn* in Whisky Park. All three of 'em turn out first-class ore. Smartest mining man in the county owns a chunk of stock in all three; about ten percent interest in each mine, they say. He's hangin' on to it till the Moffatt line gets here."

"Yeh? Who is he?"

"Broker and mineral expert named Kincaid. He's got faith in that Hahn's Peak district; figures there'll be a big boom up there once they shorten the ore haul."

"On the level, is he?" Otto prodded.

"Far as I know he is. I had an old played-out claim myself, year or so ago. Got Kincaid to sell it for me and he fetched me a fair price; only charged me six percent commission."

"Does he inspect and appraise mining properties?"

"Sure. Charges by the day when he does that. But a fair charge, they say. You're likely to find him riding a mule all over the top end of Routt County, lookin' over claims."

For what it was worth, Bundchu filed the information in a corner of his mind.

At supper he again saw the girl, Verna, at a table with the man she called Mr. Garrison. He appeared to be in his middle thirties, the girl more than ten years younger. Watching them covertly,

Otto got the impression that Garrison didn't quite ring true. He couldn't pin it down. But for the last ten years Otto Bundchu had been associating daily with convicted criminals. It had given him a sixth sense for distinguishing them from other people. On the surface Garrison was a man more than commonly personable, trying to make himself liked by an exceptionally attractive girl. She'd be sorry, Otto guessed, if she let him get away with it.

It was only a hunch, based on rubbing shoulders for a long time with the wrong kind of men.

After dinner what he wanted most was a whisky and soda—a luxury denied him in the long years of his prison life. No liquor to be had, the hotel porter told him, unless he wanted to take a walk over the river bridge. Steamboat itself was bone dry.

Just before bedtime Otto took the walk. The bridge was dark as he crossed it, and he could understand how easy it had been for someone to waylay Yancy here. He hurried on to the saloon row known as Brooklyn.

It had changed a little since he'd seen it ten years ago. Three saloons now instead of two. Back of them Bonnie's Place was still there, ablaze with lights. Every hitchrail had horses. In Big John's a banjo player was singing while customers stomped and clapped hands.

Otto had a drink at John's bar and then moved

on to Bart Tarkio's next door. Two women from Bonnie's were perched on stools there and one of them smiled invitingly as Otto came in. To avoid her he backed out and went on to the third saloon, Jeffry Silverton's.

At the rear of the barroom five men were playing poker. Otto blinked when he saw that one of them was the mining broker, Ambrose Kincaid. Most of the chips on the table were stacked in front of Kincaid.

Otto went only to the front of the bar, where he ordered a highball. Over it he worked up casual talk with the customer at his elbow. "Isn't that Gregg Griggs playing poker back there? I mean the guy with the short pointed beard."

The man looked and shook his head. "Nope; that's Ambrose Kincaid. Comes over here about two evenings a week, Kincaid does."

"Likes his liquor?"

"No more than the next man. Never knew him to take too many. Likes a friendly game of draw, now and then. Purty good at it too. Usually comes out ahead."

Without letting himself be seen by Kincaid, Otto went home and to bed. Not counting what he'd been told by a cellmate, he now knew three things about Kincaid. He had a good reputation here in Routt County. He had faith in the future of the Hahn's Peak mining district and had proved it by investing in three of its leading mines. And he went over to Brooklyn several evenings a week, mainly for a hand at poker—a game at which he usually won.

What did it add up to? For one thing, Otto decided, it added up to opportunity. Kincaid could have been the man spotted by Yancy—who'd followed Yancy to an undersheriff's office and then waited for him on a dark river bridge. And as a mine appraiser who sometimes rode through the hills north of here, he could have passed through Slater Park on the day of Lassiter's murder.

No one else around here would think such thoughts about Ambrose Kincaid. But no one else around here had been tipped off by a recent cellmate of Otto's to the fact, for instance, that this same Ambrose Kincaid under another name had once been a dealer at the Oriental gambling resort in Tombstone, Arizona, with the reputation of dealing off the bottom of a deck.

Before going to sleep, Otto Bundchu decided to call at Kincaid's office tomorrow and offer himself as a client.

VII

When he went in to breakfast in the morning, he saw at once that the girl Verna had changed escorts. She was at a table with two range-clad cowboys, while the man Garrison sat alone across the room. Both cowboys looked to be under thirty, one tall and black-haired, the other blocky and blond. Each wore spurred boots, denims, and a leather jacket. The girl seemed definitely to like them and was calling them Wayne and Jim.

The long center table was empty, the regular boarders who ate there having gone about their day's affairs. Bits of talk came to Otto from the girl and her companions.

"When do you expect your uncle back, Verna?"

"On today's stage, I hope. His last case of the session was heard yesterday. After he comes I won't be a lady of leisure any more. I'll have two jobs: his office girl and his housekeeper."

"Jim and I," the black-haired man said, "want to have a little pow-wow with him when he shows up."

A well-fed townsman of middle age came in and hung his hat on a rack. Bundchu took him for a prosperous merchant or banker. A waitress spoke to him. "Where would you like to sit, Mr.

Barnett? Mr. Garrison looks lonesome all by himself. Would you like to . . . ?"

Mr. Barnett definitely didn't like to. Otto saw him look at Garrison with an expression of something between distaste and loathing. He chose a table as far away from Garrison as he could get. Some personal feud, Otto supposed.

After breakfast Bundchu idled an hour in the lobby, skimming through a Denver paper which someone had tossed aside. The main news in it was about the Moffatt line. There were hot rumours that it would build the longest tunnel in America through the range to connect Middle Park with Steamboat Springs—and then on to Salt Lake City.

Bundchu doubted it. It was probably a boomer plant to hike land prices west of the divide.

At exactly ten o'clock he walked three blocks down Lincoln to the Seventh Street corner. Steep narrow steps took him to an upper hallway which gave to offices. The front office had Ambrose Kincaid's name on it. Bundchu went in without knocking.

The man with the short pointed beard sat at his desk writing a report. He finished a paragraph, then looked up with a bland smile. "Yes?" His tone and his calm, level gaze made it clear that he hadn't the least idea that his caller was the notorious Otto Bundchu.

A table of quartz samples stood in a corner. The

74

walls had maps—a complete map of Routt County and a map of the Hahn's Peak mining district showing the more important claims there.

"You sell mining properties on commission?" Otto asked.

"Sometimes." Kincaid waved him to a chair. "You got one to sell?"

Otto nodded. "What commission do you charge?"

"The usual. Six percent."

"I'm prepared to pay twice that, Mr. Kincaid. Twelve percent; because this particular sale will require a little extra effort."

Kincaid opened a box of cigars, offered one to his client. "I don't smoke," Otto told him. "Got out of the habit these last ten years."

The broker trimmed his cigar and lighted it. The term "ten years" gave a hint of the caller's identity but Kincaid, completely off guard, missed it.

"This mine property you speak of—it's in the Hahn's Peak district, I take it."

"That's right." Abruptly Otto added: "But I'm the only man in the world who can go to it. Did you ever hear of Karl Janvers? You didn't know him, naturally. He died before you came to this neck of the woods."

Kincaid's jaw dropped and for a minute he sat staring. "The only man alive," he said slowly, "who could go to the Janvers strike is Otto Bundchu. *You?*"

"Yes. Me. I'm the only one who knows where it is. But if you'll be my broker, Kincaid, there'll be two of us. You and me."

Kincaid's cigar went out. He was now tense and wary—with a feeling that a trap was about to be set for him. Here was a man who'd been convicted of murdering Janvers and who'd paid the penalty for it. At the very least, he'd be a dangerous man to deal with.

Ambrose Kincaid mopped a handkerchief across a damp forehead before speaking. "Am I right in assuming you'll now go to the Janvers gulch, stake a gold claim there, and as soon as you have it recorded you'll turn it over to me for sale?"

Bundchu shook his head. "Not quite. I'm not going to the place myself for three good reasons."

When he listed the three reasons, to Kincaid they seemed logical and convincing.

"So my proposition is this," Otto went on. "I have a map of the place in my pocket. I turn it over to you, and with it you can easily find the spot. Nobody at Hahn's Peak will follow you there. They're used to seeing you ride off into the hills on some routine appraisal or promotion errand. Once you get to the gulch you stake a claim along it, fifteen hundred feet long by six hundred feet wide. That'll cover the cream of the pay gravel. Then you ride back to the courthouse, and to the mineral commissioner's office, and record the claim in my name.

"As soon as the title is properly recorded in my name, you send me the certificate by mail. I'll be at the Windsor Hotel in Denver. After that you advertize the claim for sale and sell it at a fair price, which you collect and send to me at Denver after deducting a twelve percent fee for yourself. Is that clear?"

To Ambrose Kincaid it was reasonably clear except for one thing. Being a draw poker player used to laying cards face up on the table, he did so now. "I'm a stranger to you, Bundchu. So why do you trust me? What's to keep me from filing the claim in my own name, recording it in my name, and leaving you clear out of it?"

Otto smiled. "I expected you to bring that up. My protection is the name you're going to give to the claim. Every mine has a name. You own stock in three of them yourself, I'm told; the *Tom Thum*, the *Elkhorn*, and the *Minnie D.* So I instruct you now to give a name of my own choice to the claim you'll file in the Janvers gulch."

Again Kincaid stared. "Yeh? What name have you got in mind?"

"Let's call it the *Little Joe.*"

For a minute the name had no particular significance to Kincaid. He'd heard the term used to describe a throw of dice—a pair of deuces. "Okay," he agreed cautiously. "So we call it the *Little Joe.* Big Joe or Little Joe, how does that protect you from a double cross?"

"Little Joe," Otto reminded him, "was a bartender in the Oriental Saloon and gambling hall run by Wyatt Earp at Tombstone, Arizona, twenty years ago. Later he came to Colorado and joined up with some bad company in Brown's Park, west end of this county. There was a gunfight with a posse and Little Joe was picked up. They gave him a life term at Canon City."

The trap was sprung, and the sudden grayness on Kincaid's face showed that he knew it. He himself, long ago, had been a dealer at the Oriental and now he vaguely remembered a small, bald bartender they'd called Little Joe.

"You don't have to take my word for it," Otto said. "Little Joe was tried and convicted at Hahn's Peak three years ago. Joseph Benny was his name. You probably read about in the Steamboat Springs weeklies, but you wouldn't connect Joseph Benny of Brown's Park with Little Joe a Tombstone bartender. But while waiting trial at Hahn's Peak Little Joe saw you and knew you; he saw you again as he passed through Steamboat by stagecoach on his way to prison.

"I'd been in Canon City six years when he got there. When I heard he'd come via Hahn's Peak, the same as me, I looked him up. Later they let us share a cell and we got to be buddies."

After a long heavy silence Kincaid asked, "Just what do you want, Bundchu?"

"I've already told you," Otto insisted. "I want

you to stake a claim for me, record it in my name, sell it for a fair price and then help yourself to a twelve percent commission. That's all there is to it."

"And what would you call a fair price?"

Otto shrugged. "That's your department. I'm not a mining broker; you are. But we both know this. That gulch is so rich that Janvers by himself with nine months' panning took about thirty thousand in gold out of it. Everybody else knows it too. You'll get offers based on that fact."

From an inner pocket he took a sketch made last night in his hotel room and gave it to Kincaid. It covered an area at the head of Oliver Creek about six miles west and two miles north of Hahn's Peak and half a mile south of a conspicuous pinnacle called "The Nipple."

"The Janvers pay gravel," Otto explained, "runs along that creek from a lightning-struck lodge-pole pine snag to an outcrop of red sandstone six hundred paces downgulch. There's a knothole in the pine snag eight feet above ground, and you'll have to stand on your saddled mule to reach it. If you'll put your hand into that knothole you'll find a rusty bean can with my name on it. Knowing that much, and with this sketch in hand, you can't miss it."

Kincaid could hardly believe it. This was an area in which no gold strikes had ever been reported. All the known pay strikes had been north and east of Hahn's Peak—not west. "It doesn't make sense!" he protested. "Nobody ever . . ."

He stopped as he remembered something. According to ten-year-old news accounts, Janvers' body had been found under a brush-pile on Middle Fork of the Little Snake; his horse and pack mare had been found grazing just north and east of Shield Mountain. Those areas were only a little way north of the Nipple.

"Go look and see," Bundchu said. "And don't forget my address; after this week it'll be the Windsor Hotel, Denver."

Cocksure that Kincaid would "go look and see," Otto left the office and headed for the Sheridan.

When he got there the daily stage from Hahn's Peak was just pulling in. A lanky lawyer with a bony, Lincolnesque face got off and was met by three people who stood on the walk waiting for him. The girl Verna threw her arms around his neck and kissed him and called him Uncle Nate. Back of her stood two cowboys, and presently one of them said, "Thanks for getting me off, Mr. Bainbridge."

The other cowboy said, "Could we see you some time today, Mr. Bainbridge, whenever you have time?"

"You sure can, Brady," the lawyer agreed. "Drop in at my office this afternoon. If I'm not there, sit down and wait for me."

The law office was empty when Wayne and Jim

called there in midafternoon. They went in to wait. They could tell that Verna had been here this morning to tidy up. The place was dustless, with a vase of flowers on the desk and with accumulated mail stacked neatly.

Presently the attorney came in. "Sorry I'm late. Had to show my niece up to the cottage where I've been baching these last few years. Right away she pitched in to clean the place up. You boys are not in any trouble, I hope."

"No law trouble," Jim Gentry said. "Just trouble finding a job." He told about the U Bar backing away after having first offered him work. "It'll be that way everywhere till we find out who took Mark Lassiter's money."

"I'm seeing it through with him," Wayne added. "Maybe you can help us."

"How?"

"Jim says he once heard his boss mention you as his lawyer. Were you?"

"I drew a will for him, year or so ago. He left it in my safe. Matter of fact, that's the only time I ever saw him."

"Who gets his property?" Jim Gentry asked.

"An orphanage at Fort Smith, Arkansas. Mark Lassiter was a ward there through most of his childhood. I don't think he had any living relative."

"We've been trying to figure out," Wayne said, "why anyone would want Lassiter dead."

"You can rule out an inheritance motive," the

lawyer assured them. "No one profits by his death except the Arkansas orphanage. I wrote them asking what disposition they want made of the estate, once it's probated." Bainbridge began thumbing through a stack of accumulated mail. "Let's see if there's an answer. Yes, here it is."

He opened a letter with a Fort Smith postmark. After skimming through it he summed up: "They instruct me to put a caretaker on the ranch for the time being, just to make sure that vandals don't come along and haul away stuff like saddles, harness, and furniture. After probate they'd like to have the property sold for their benefit."

"It's our idea," Brady said, "that two men went to Lassiter's place that day. A killer and a thief." He sketched the theory outlined by the stage driver, George Wren. "The killer could be a Brooklyn toughie who wanted Lassiter shut up, for one reason or another. After he did it maybe someone else came along and robbed the money cache."

The attorney gave a grave nod. "Makes sense, after what happened to Old Man Yancy on the bridge."

"And with the woman Mattie gettin' scared," Jim put in, "after findin' out what happened to my boss. We talked it over with Undersheriff Camp and he thinks George Wren's got the right slant on it."

Bainbridge regarded them quizzically. "As I

understand it, you boys are out to clear Jim's name. The way to do it is to turn up both the killer and the thief. Have you made any progress?"

"We've made the rounds of the livery barns," Brady told him. "Three barns in Steamboat, none in Brooklyn. If a Brooklyn toughie rode to Slater Park, he'd likely need to rent a saddle horse. He'd be gone about two days—a day going up and a day coming back. We asked each livery stable to take a look at their books and see who rented a saddle horse for about forty hours at the time of Lassiter's murder."

"A sharp idea," Bainbridge approved. "What did they say?"

"A blind haul at two barns. But at the Reinhart barn on Ninth Street the book says that Dale Garrison rented a horse the day before it happened and kept it out two days."

"I've met Garrison," Bainbridge said. "Seems respectable enough. Goes with the right people. No connection with the Brooklyn crowd, far as I know. Been living at the Sheridan Hotel for the last year or so. They say he's looking for a ranch property."

"Lassiter," Brady pointed out, "was advertizing his ranch for sale. Garrison could have ridden up for a look. But he claims he didn't."

"You braced him?"

Brady nodded. "We went right from Reinhart's stable to see him. Asked him where he rode that livery horse those two days. He had an answer and it seems to check out."

"What did he say?"

"Says he's bid on three or four Routt County properties and always got outbid. Then he thought maybe he could do better up in Idaho. He knows a cowboy named Bart Conroy who used to ride for Idaho outfits. So he rode up to Conroy's homestead at the head of Mill Creek. That's about two-thirds of the way to Slater Park. He figured to ask Conroy about Idaho land properties and if it's a good cow country. But Conroy wasn't home. It was past sundown and Garrison says he stayed all night there. Hung around most of the next day waiting for Conroy to show up, then rode back to Steamboat. Conroy happens to be in town today and I checked with him. He says when he got back from a hay job he saw that someone had spent the night in his cabin. It was the right night. Like as not it was Garrison." ·

"Which doesn't prove," Jim Gentry argued, "that Garrison didn't go on to Slater Park. Only thing is, he's a softie. I mean he's no hard-case gun-toter. More at home in a parlor, I'd say, than in a ranch yard prowling for a dead man's money."

Brady took it from there. "I'd figure him the same way, Jim, except for what happened on a stagecoach coming over from Wolcott."

"You were on the stage with him?" Bainbridge prompted.

"Yes, and so was your niece Verna. She sat between me and Garrison on the back seat. He kept up a rapid-fire chatter most of the night. Then at the Yampa stop I picked up a Steamboat Springs paper and learned for the first time about what happened at Slater Park. The stage pulled out with Garrison as gabby as ever—until I started to tell Verna about Mark Lassiter. She asked questions—but Garrison didn't. Not a peep out of him for the next couple of hours."

"Which still doesn't prove anything," Jim muttered.

"No," Wayne admitted. "But it starts you thinking after you find out about Garrison riding north on a rented horse and gone two days."

Bainbridge weighed the facts shrewdly. "He'll bear watching, this man Garrison. So why don't you watch him, Brady. Keep an eye on him for a while. He lives at the Sheridan, and you can take a room there yourself."

"For my money," Jim Gentry argued, "the guys to watch are those buckos over at Brooklyn. It was somebody at Brooklyn who killed Old Man Yancy. And the same somebody must've killed Lassiter."

"Okay," the attorney agreed. "So why don't you split up? Let Brady stay at the Sheridan and watch Garrison. And Jim, you could rent one of those bunks up over Big John's saloon across the river. You could hang around all three barrooms and see what you can pick up."

Jim and Wayne exchanged glances and both nodded. "We'll do that, Mr. Bainbridge. Thanks for the idea." In a moment Brady added: "Speaking of ideas, I've got one myself. If you need a caretaker to put on the Slater Park ranch for a while, what about old Walt Cody? He's a retired stage driver at a loose end right now. Nothing he'd like better than a cabin in the woods with plenty of deer and trout and grouse close by. Honest as daylight. Handy with a gun, too, if any prowlers come around."

"I know him well," the lawyer said. "Tell him to drop in and see me." He stood up to shake hands. "Good luck, boys; if you turn up anything, let me know."

VIII

In midafternoon Brady sat in the Sheridan lobby reading the current issue of the Steamboat *Pilot*. Presently he saw a thin, pale, balding man stop at the desk and ask for his key.

The clerk gave it to him. "Here you are, Mr. Bundchu. Been over to the bath house again, have you?"

"That's what I came here for," the man said. "It sort of picks me up. While I think of it, I'll be checking out Saturday. Please reserve a seat for me on Saturday's stage to Wolcott. If any mail comes after that, you can forward it to the Windsor Hotel in Denver."

"Very well, Mr. Bundchu."

The man went upstairs, and Brady, although he'd never seen him before, now knew who he was. The newspaper had a column about him. He was a released convict who'd arrived here a few days ago; and although everyone had expected him to go to Hahn's Peak and file a mining claim, he'd surprised them by saying he'd come only for the mineral baths and would be leaving shortly for the Outside.

The paper reviewed the sensational ten-year-old story about the murder of Karl Janvers and the conviction of Bundchu.

But Brady's concern was Dale Garrison, and there could hardly be a connection between Garrison and Bundchu.

The clerk left the room on some errand, and Brady strolled over for a look at the registry book. He wanted to find out the number of Garrison's room. It wasn't on the open page, but Bundchu's was. Bundchu had room 209. Permanent boarders like Garrison weren't listed here. But when Brady turned back to the first page of the book he found a list of regulars who paid by the month. Garrison's name was there, and his room was 206.

It put him right across the hall from Brady, who had number 208.

Back of the desk was a key rack with the 206 hook empty. The key was probably in Garrison's pocket. Brady was determined to search the room at the first opportunity, hoping for a tip to the man's background.

There should be a master key around the desk somewhere, which the clerk or porter could use in an emergency. He looked behind the desk and saw a hook with a single key on it. More than likely a master key which would open any room.

Brady stepped away quickly when he heard someone come in from the street. It was the old ex–stage driver, Walt Cody. Brady met him heartily. "You're just the man I want to see, Walt. How would you like a nice soft caretaker job up in Slater Park?"

"Lead me to it. Who'd I be workin' for?"

"Go see Nathan Bainbridge and he'll tell you. They want someone to keep an eye on the Lassiter ranch for a while."

"Lots of pin-tail grouse up that way," Cody said. "And a crikful of natives. I'd be livin' high till snow flies."

As he started out Brady followed him to the front walk. "One more thing, Walt. What do you know about Dale Garrison?"

The old-timer cocked an eye. "What's he got to do with Slater Park?"

"Nothing, far as I know. He was on the stage with us, remember?"

"Yeh. Shinin' up to that good-lookin' gal. Claims to be in the market fer a cow ranch. He's looked at a lot of 'em, but he never closed a deal."

"Any idea where he came from?"

"Never heard him say. Back east somewhere, likely. I better go see Bainbridge before somebody else grabs that job."

Cody went off down the street and Brady turned back into the lobby. The clerk was behind the desk again and spoke to a roomer coming down the stairs. "Your laundry came, Mr. Garrison. I'll send it up to your room."

"Thanks, Dave." Garrison gave a careless salute to Wayne Brady and went out the street door.

Half a minute later, Brady went out to follow him. He had no plan except to learn all he could about the man's habits and connections. He saw Garrison exchange greetings with people he passed on the walk, then turn in at the post office. Brady stood a distance away, waiting for him to come out.

Emerging from the post office Garrison almost collided with a stylishly dressed woman who was about to go in. Garrison obviously knew her; he bowed politely and tipped his hat. But the woman moved coldly by him with her chin high. As frigid a snub as Brady had ever seen!

Town Marshal Burgess stood nearby, and

Brady asked curiously: "That lady over there." He pointed to the woman who'd just cold-shouldered Garrison. "Who is she?"

Burgess grinned. "Where 've you been, Brady? Don't reckon you get to town very often. She's the top society lady around here. Mrs. Abner Barnett. Her husband owns the biggest store in Routt County."

A memory pricked Brady. At breakfast in the dining room Abner Barnett himself had declined a waitress' suggestion that he share a table with Garrison. What did the Barnetts have against Dale Garrison?

The man was now heading easterly along the walk. Brady saw him turn in at the Excelsior Billiard Parlor. A minute later Brady looked in there and saw him start a billiard game with one of the idlers. It should occupy them half an hour. A chance, Brady decided, to search Garrison's room at the Sheridan.

He hurried back there and had to wait in the lobby only a few minutes before the clerk again vacated the desk on some errand. Brady promptly helped himself to a master key and went up to the second-floor corridor. The key fit when he tried it in the lock of Number 206. It was a cheap lock. Probably any standard skeleton key bought at a hardware store would do just as well.

Brady went in and closed the door softly. A chambermaid had tidied the room. He crossed to the window and pulled the shade part-way down. It still left enough daylight filtering in for his purpose.

There was a bed, a table, a dresser, a desk, and a small table with an oil lamp on it. A number of expensive suits were on hangers in a closet. A recent copy of the *Rocky Mountain News* reminded Brady that Garrison had returned from Denver only a few days ago. Near it lay a month-old copy of *Leslie's Weekly.* A rack of current novels indicated that Garrison was something of a reader.

Was he also a criminal? If so he'd own a gun, Brady thought, and he began a search for one. The closet had two travelling bags, which he opened and found empty. He went through every dresser drawer and found nothing out of the ordinary. Certainly there was no gun in the room.

He went back to the closet and searched pockets of every garment hanging there. Again it was a blind haul. The travelling bags had no secret pouches or false bottoms. A man of normal habits and background would have a few old letters or bills or receipts. In the desk drawers Brady found no letters or bills. The only receipt was for the rent of this room.

It struck Garrison as odd that these personal possessions of Garrison offered absolutely no hint of his past. If anyone would go through his own things, at the Cary ranch bunkhouse, he'd find relics of other ranch jobs held by Brady.

There'd be a family record or two, clippings, and old letters, perhaps dating back to his early boyhood.

But here there was nothing. A curtain seemed to have dropped to obscure the past life of Dale Garrison.

Brady returned to the desk and made a closer search there. Under a D. & R. G. train schedule folder he found a tiny bank book—a checking account pass book issued by the Milner Bank of Steamboat Springs. Brady opened it and saw that the account had been started about a year ago and that since then there'd been just four deposits.

Each deposit was exactly one thousand dollars. And the deposits had been made at intervals of exactly three months.

It seemed to mean that Dale Garrison had a fixed income of four thousand dollars a year, payable quarterly. Was Garrison a remittance man? A Britisher, possibly? Perhaps the black sheep younger son of some well-to-do English or Scotch family, packed off to America with the assurance that so long as he stayed there he'd be sent a quarterly remittance. Brady had run across several such remittance men out here in the west—ranging in status from idlers living in clubs at Denver and Cheyenne down to cast-off derelicts receiving only a pittance. He knew of a case where the remittance had been cut off—and the man had taken a job herding sheep.

Before putting the bank pass book back where he'd found it, Brady memorized the dates of the four deposits. Then he smoothed away all sign of his intrusion and left the room, locking the door behind him.

He crossed to his own room and there, while they were still fresh in his mind, he jotted down the dates of the four one-thousand-dollar deposits.

A sound of moving in the next room reminded him that it was Otto Bundchu's, Number 209. But his interest was in Garrison, not in Bundchu.

He went down to the lobby and found no one there except a pair of drummers playing checkers. It was a chance to return the pass key to its hook behind the registry desk, and Brady managed it without being noticed.

Going out, he headed east. When he passed a billiard hall he looked in and saw Garrison still with a cue in hand. A block further, Brady turned in at the city jail and found Undersheriff Jack Camp there.

"Anything new, Jack?"

The county officer shook his head. "Just went over to Brooklyn and checked with Jim Gentry. He's taken a bunk by the week up over Big John's bar. Tonight he'll make a round of the saloons and keep his eyes open. What about you, Brady?"

"I took a look in Garrison's room and found a bank pass book." Brady described the pass book with its four quarterly deposits.

"Sounds like a remittancer," the undersheriff agreed. "If he is, those four remittances would come in the form of a draft from London or maybe Edinburgh. Let's go check with Mr. Milner."

At the bank they were told that Mr. Milner had gone to Craig to negotiate a cattle loan. His cashier, Carpenter, looked stubborn when Cody inquired about deposits.

"You're not charging Mr. Garrison with anything, are you, Sheriff?"

"No," Camp admitted. "We think he's a remittance man from back east or maybe from overseas. If he is, that's all we want to know. Can you tell us where those four one-thousand-dollar deposits came from?"

"It's our policy not to give out information about a client's account," Carpenter said, "unless we're shown a court order. A bank considers such matters confidential."

Camp gave a shrug. "Okay. I'll send for a court order."

Outside he told Brady: "I'll get a letter off to Judge Shumate at Hahn's Peak right away. Means a delay of a couple of days. Meantime I'll leave it to you and Jim Gentry. He can keep an eye on Brooklyn while you keep an eye on Garrison."

On the way back to the Sheridan, Brady stopped at a livery barn for a look at his horse and Jim Gentry's. Jim had ridden his down from Hahn's Peak and Brady, after getting a leave of absence from the Cary brothers, had ridden his own mount up from Hayden.

For the rest of the day and until bedtime, as inconspicuously as possible he managed to keep track of Garrison's movements. They seemed routine—a haircut, a call at a real estate office to inquire about ranches for sale, lunch and supper in the hotel dining room, and a walk up Eighth Street to the Nathan Bainbridge cottage. The man was only in the cottage about ten minutes, and by his look when he came out Brady guessed he'd asked Verna for a date and failed to get it. About two hours after supper Garrison went up to his room, and Brady assumed he was settled for the night. Brady himself lingered in the lobby for another hour. Two drummers were playing Pitch and the ex-convict, Bundchu, stood looking on. A night clerk dozed back of the registry desk. The drummers invited Bundchu to sit in, and he accepted, the play going on for small stakes.

They were still playing when, at near midnight, Brady went up to his room. A long second-floor corridor leading to the rear was lighted by a bracketed oil lamp. Brady went into Room 208 and lighted his own lamp. In ten minutes he was in bed but for a while lay wakeful, wondering about the source of Garrison's quarterly income. Certainly he'd done nothing to earn it around Steamboat Springs.

Brady was still awake when again, like this

morning, he heard a sound of movement in the next room. Bundchu's room. Wall partitions were thin here at the Sheridan. He supposed that Bundchu was taking off his boots for the night . . .

But how could he? A few minutes ago Bundchu had been playing cards in the lobby. If he'd quit the game and come upstairs, why hadn't Brady heard him pass by in the hall and turn a key in the lock of his door?

The question disturbed Brady. How could anyone but Bundchu, at this late hour, be in that room?

No further sound came from it. But the doubt still nagged at Brady. It made him get out of bed and put on a bath robe and slippers. He went quietly out into the hall and looked at the glass transom over 209's door. It was dark; so no lamp was lighted in there. To Brady it didn't seem likely that Bundchu would undress in the dark.

Was he still playing cards in the lobby? Brady moved softly up the carpeted hallway to the head of the stairs. Looking down them, he could see most of the lighted lobby. Yes, three men were at cards down there, and one of them was Bundchu. Behind a registry desk a night clerk was still dozing.

Brady went back to his own room, and listened a moment for a sound from the next one. Only a midnight silence came from it. With a shrug he concluded that imagination had played him a trick. Since Bundchu himself wasn't in it, Room 209 had to be empty.

He'd better stop thinking about Bundchu and concentrate on Garrison—the man who'd made four quarterly deposits of a thousand dollars each. Three months after the last one, would a fifth one be made? What would be the exact date of it? According to the precedents, it should be ninety days after the fourth deposit. To fix the date in his mind, Brady decided to look at the memorandum he'd jotted down. No longer sleepy, he lighted his table lamp, rolled a cigaret, and picked up a coat he'd draped over a chair back. From a coat pocket he took a scrap of paper which told him that the fourth deposit had been made on the 16th of June.

So the next one would normally be made on the 16th of September—still a month away. Long before that, with the help of a court order, they would have learned the source of the man's income.

Brady turned out the lamp, then sat down to finish his cigaret. He wasn't quite done with it when he heard someone come up from the lobby and head this way along the hall. It would be Bundchu, probably, coming late to bed.

The footsteps stopped at Bundchu's door, and Brady heard a key turn in the lock. He heard the door open and close as Bundchu went into his room.

The next three sounds were sharp, arresting,

ominous—and brought Wayne Brady alertly to his feet. They were a thump, a muffled outcry, followed by another thump or thud.

After that, silence.

The meaning of the sequence of sounds seemed clear to Brady. Someone had been in there waiting for Bundchu—perhaps for all of the last hour. Someone who'd stood in the dark with a club or gun in hand. A bang on the head, bringing an outcry from Bundchu, then a second thump as the victim hit the floor.

By the time he'd reasoned that far, Brady had dashed out into the hallway, where he'd be able to see the assailant as he retreated from Room 209. Unless he dropped from a second floor window, the only route of escape would be through the hallway door.

But no one came out, and there was no further sound from the room. Nor had the scuffle alerted anyone from the lobby or from other rooms along this hallway. After a minute of silence Brady decided that the man was waiting to be sure of it before coming out. There was a door at the rear of the hallway which gave to alley steps. Almost certainly he'd come in that way, and planned to escape by the same route.

Another half-minute of quiet made Brady wonder if the man might not be stooping over a stunned victim to search his pockets. What for? Maybe for a clew or sketch which could reveal the location of a gold gulch known only to Bundchu.

The door must still be unlocked. Bundchu had had no time to relock it before being struck down. Moving forward, Brady tried the knob of it. The knob turned and the door gave to his push. Still no sound came from the other side of it. Wayne Brady pushed the door halfway open. The room beyond was completely dark.

From a pocket of his dressing robe Brady fished a match, struck it, held it in front of him for a few seconds, then snuffed it out. In the brief flare he'd seen Bundchu, lying either stunned or dead, on the floor just inside the room. Nothing else. And still no sound. The man who'd waylaid him could be standing in darkness with his back to a wall, or hiding in the room's closet.

What Brady needed was a gun. There was a town ordinance directing that guns must be left with the town marshal, or at a livery stable, by any armed rider coming into Steamboat Springs. Brady had left his own gun wrapped in his blanket roll at the Reinhart stable.

Surely the man in this dark room had a gun, but Brady had a feeling he wouldn't risk shooting. A shot would draw other people from the second floor rooms and from the lobby, and maybe even from the street. For that reason the man in there hadn't shot Otto Bundchu, but had merely clubbed him down.

But Wayne Brady had an advantage over

Bundchu. Bundchu had entered carelessly, not expecting an attack. Brady expected one and was ready. He wasn't afraid of a scuffle either in darkness or light, and he didn't believe there'd be a shot. Even if the man shot at him, he'd be shooting in the dark.

Bending low, Brady moved quickly into the room and then dodged to one side. No sound came from the other man. It might be that he'd already escaped by dropping from a window. The drop would only be about twelve feet to a vacant lot.

Brady fished out a second match. In three fast movements he lighted it, tossed it into the middle of the room, and then slipped a little way along the wall. Again the brief flare revealed nothing except the form of a man lying dead or stunned on the floor.

After another minute of stillness Brady concluded that the assailant, if he hadn't escaped by the window, was hiding in the room's closet. He may not have heard Brady come in; or he might be waiting for Brady to go down to the lobby to raise an alarm, giving the man a chance to slip out into the hall and then leave by the alley exit.

All the hotel rooms were more or less alike, so Brady knew that the closet would be in the same corner as the one in his own room. He began groping toward it, hands reaching out in front of him. One groping step, two, three . . .

He was taking the fourth step when something

hard and heavy, maybe a gun, banged down on his head. It was a glancing blow, sliding down the side of his face with a sharp slap at his ear. As he whirled about, the other man grappled with him in the dark.

Brady wrenched from the clinch, got his right arm free and swung blindly at where he thought a face should be. The swing landed on flesh, maybe a cheek or a neck, and at the same moment he heard a moaning sound which came not from his adversary but from Bundchu on the floor. It was a moan that seemed to be the single syllable "Oh!" but Brady was too occupied with his struggle to be certain of it. An instant later a knee bumped him in the groin, and again the barrel of a gun crashed down on his head.

This time Brady went to his knees, and before he could cry out a third blow hit the top of his head and flattened him. He was down and out for half-a-minute.

His first awareness after he came to and got groggily to his feet was of voices in the hallway. Doors were opening along the corridor. Footsteps came running up from the lobby. Then the roomer in 205 came in, holding a lighted lamp. It exposed Bundchu on the floor and Brady staggering to his feet with blood on his skull and face.

The hall was full of voices, and others peered in, including the night clerk. Manager Harry Monson came down the hall, shouting questions. A man pointed to the rear door which gave to alley steps. "He went that way," the man reported.

"You saw him?"

"Only his back as he went out."

There was a rush to the hallway exit. Brady himself joined it, still unsteady on his legs. The door opened to exterior steps which went steeply down to an inky dark alley. Whoever had escaped that way was now long-gone.

The roomer who'd had a glimpse of him hadn't seen him frontally. "Might be anyone," he admitted.

Definitely it wasn't Dale Garrison. Garrison in his nightshirt stood in the doorway of his room, rubbing sleepy eyes.

In Room 209, now lamp-lighted, a man stooped over Otto Bundchu. "He's stopped breathing," the man reported. "Somebody bashed him on the head."

Town Marshal Burgess came dashing along the hall and into Room 209. After a look he said grimly: "Otto Bundchu, huh? He had it coming, maybe. Karl Janvers had plenty of friends and looks like one of 'em figured to get even."

IX

By morning the news was all over town, and almost to a man the town jumped to the same conclusion. Who else but some old-timer from Hahn's Peak could it be? What other reason than revenge for the murder of Karl Janvers?

All morning knots of men stood on the sidewalks recalling memories of the trial ten years ago—a trial at the Hahn's Peak courtroom and the unpopular verdict. Big John had run a saloon there then, and a score of Karl Janvers' friends had been lining the bar when word came that Bundchu had been let off with only a prison term.

"He'd orter be hanged!" had been the explosive reaction. "Sneak-killing Karl and then jumping his claim!"

"I was at the Peak myself that day," Undersheriff Jack Camp remembered. "There was plenty of lynch talk, and we had to scoot Otto out of town under cover of darkness and hustle him off to the Canon City pen."

Later in the morning, Wayne Brady, after a bruise on his cheek had been treated by Doctor Solandt, went to the city jail and heard Camp repeat that conclusion. The undersheriff looked up grimly. "How's your head, Brady?"

"Aching." Brady gave a grimace. "I deserve it, letting him get away like that."

"You say you clinched with him," Camp prodded. "What did he feel like? Thick, skinny, tall, or short?"

"Medium, I'd say; but I can't be sure. I never saw him. It was pitch dark. I got in one swipe, and I think it hit his cheek or neck. Maybe it left a mark."

A man from the *Pilot* was there. "Do you agree with Jack?" he prompted, "that some old friend of Janvers did it to get even?"

"Could be," Brady said cautiously. "But ten years is a long time for anyone to stay mad. I mean mad enough to kill. Yet one thing does sorta make it look that way."

"Yeh? What?"

"When Bundchu came straight here from prison, everyone expected him to go on to Hahn's Peak and file a gold claim in the Janvers gulch. But he fooled us. He got off at Steamboat and said he'd hang around a few days, take some mineral baths and then head back for the Outside. Sounds kinda phony, I'd say."

"Struck me the same way," the *Pilot* man agreed.

"My hunch is," Brady went on, "that he remembered the lynch talk at the end of his trial ten years ago. It'd make him leery about going back to the Peak. So maybe he decided to lay over here a few days with his eyes and ears open. If no one threatened him, or talked tough, he'd take a chance and go on to the Peak."

Camp gave a thoughtful nod. "I getcha, Brady. What he saw or heard must 've scared him. Like if some old-timer came up and told him to get to hell outa Routt County. So he reserved a seat on Saturday's coach for the Outside. Figured his life was worth more than all the gold in that gulch."

"But before Saturday came," the *Pilot* man added, "he got clubbed down in the dark."

The undersheriff chased everyone but Brady out of the office, and the two went into a huddle. "Makes three killings in all: Lassiter, Yancy, Bundchu. It's a cinch the same man knocked off Lassiter and Yancy. Question is—did the same man kill Bundchu?"

Brady asked, "Have you checked with Jim this morning?"

"First thing I did. Went over to Brooklyn and shook down all three saloonmen. Got a list of eleven Hahn's Peak old-timers who've stopped by for drinks the last few days. Jim helped me. We've got Burgess out checkin' on 'em right now. Some have got bunks over at Brooklyn; some are in rooming houses over here; some are camped on the river."

Presently Town Marshal Burgess came in with a report. "All but three are in the clear, Jack. I mean they can prove where they were at midnight. Billy Hoy, Hobe Utter, and Hard-Rock Corcoran can't. Hoy's the only one with a jail record. He busted a man's jaw in a saloon fight at Columbine last year. Served six months for it. But everyone of those old-timers say the same thing about Bundchu."

"What's that?"

"They all say he had it coming. Corcoran says: 'When you find out who did it, let me know. I'll buy him a drink.' "

Camp asked, "Were any of those three in town the night Yancy was killed?"

"Only one of 'em, far as I can find out. Billy Hoy was seen at Big John's that night. Rest of 'em were up at Hahn's Peak."

The undersheriff looked at his watch. "Speaking of Hahn's Peak, the stage from there is due in ten minutes. The court order I asked for oughta be on it. Let's meet it."

He was waiting with Brady on the Sheridan Hotel walk when the coach pulled in. Bill Marshman was driving, and he handed a sealed envelope to Camp. "Sheriff Farnham said for me to deliver it personally, Jack. He'll be down himself, tomorrow."

The envelope had Judge Shumate's seal on it and contained the court order. After a glance Camp turned to Brady. "Let's go flash it on Milner."

At the bank Mr. Milner looked at the order and

106

with a shrug complied. "The four deposits Garrison made," he divulged, "were in cash. Each deposit was ten one-hundred-dollar bills."

"Did he say where he got 'em?"

"No, and we didn't ask."

Camp spoke to Wayne Brady. "Okay. So let's *us* ask him."

They found Garrison in the Sheridan lobby. "Look, Garrison," Camp said bluntly, "we're not charging you with anything. We're just curious."

"Curious about what?" Garrison appeared calm, natural, self-assured; certainly not in any way brazen. Brady got the idea that he expected questions and had prepared himself for them.

"About four cash deposits," Camp told him, "in Milner's bank. An even thousand banked there every three months. Where did the money come from?"

Garrison seemed no more disturbed than if they'd asked him the time of day. "Don't see that it's any of your business, Sheriff. But if you *must* know, it came from Diamond Dan Jackson of Denver. If you don't believe it, ask him."

Almost everyone in Colorado had heard of Diamond Dan Jackson. A sometime gambler, promoter, speculator, and a familiar figure along Holliday Street in the state's capital: sometimes rich, sometimes broke, always flashy. He was an enormously fat man who usually wore diamond shirt studs, tie-pins, and rings.

"Why," Camp queried, "would he send you a thousand dollars every three months?"

The response came glibly. "Because about a year ago I was in a stud game with him at Denver. When the game broke up, he owed me five thousand. He gave me a thousand in cash and four IOU's due three months apart. He never welshed on them. Anyone on Holliday Street 'll tell you his IOU's are as good as gold. Ask him, and he'll back me up."

The undersheriff gave him a hard stare. "How can I ask him, Garrison, when he's six feet underground? Let's have a look at that Denver paper you've been reading."

Camp picked up a week-old copy of the Denver *Rocky Mountain News*, which lay on Garrison's knees. He flipped to an inner page. "Happens I read this paper myself the other day. Here's a story about Diamond Dan Jackson. Says he dropped dead from heart failure a few days ago, account of being sixty pounds overweight."

Garrison still kept calm. He raised an eyebrow. "Did he? First I heard of it. Guess I'm lucky he paid off that fourth and last IOU."

Camp gave a shrug of frustration. There was no way to disprove Garrison's statement. His witness was a dead man; and dead men neither lie nor tell the truth.

As he walked back to the jail with Brady, Camp said moodily: "If he hadn't named Jackson he could have named any other well-to-do man who died since the fourth quarterly payment. All he had to do was read the obit columns in the papers."

"Even if Jackson sent the payments," Brady ventured, "he wouldn't send cash by stagecoach mail. A cash package like that would come by Wells-Fargo express."

When they checked at the Wells-Fargo office, there was no record of four packages from Denver addressed to Dale Garrison on or about the four deposit dates. "So he's a liar by the clock," Camp complained, "but we can't prove it."

They parted company when they came opposite steps leading up to the Bainbridge law office. "I'll run up and see if he's got any new ideas, Jack."

Brady was hoping that Verna would be there, and she was. So was her uncle. Both of them had eager questions. They'd heard, of course, about the murder in Room 209 and about Brady's scuffle with the murderer. Bruises on his left cheek and ear confirmed it.

"It's a miracle," Verna exclaimed, "that he didn't kill you too. You unarmed and he with a gun!"

"You didn't see him?" Bainbridge probed.

"Not in the dark. I clinched with him half a minute, that's all. And slapped him once on the neck and face."

"So you can't identify him," Bainbridge brooded. "But he may *think* you can. He knows you had a good feel of him. He doesn't know you were out for a minute. He had to open the door to get out into a lamp-lighted hall. If you'd been conscious you'd have seen him limned against the hall light as he went out. He doesn't know you didn't get to your feet and run out into the hall in time to see him skip out the alley door."

"I wouldn't have seen anything but his back."

"But he can't be sure of that," the lawyer argued. "We know what he does to people who can point a finger at him. He shuts them up. He did it to Yancy, Bundchu—and maybe to Lassiter. If he thinks you can point a finger, you're likely to be put on his list."

To Verna it was a frightening prospect. "I wish you'd stay away from that awful place across the river, Wayne. What do they call it—Brooklyn?"

"Brooklyn's Jim Gentry's department," Wayne told her. "Anyway we've got no proof the guy's a Brooklynite. He could be anyone in town."

"The way it looks," Bainbridge summed up, "we're dealing with two criminals: a killer and a thief—the man who murdered Lassiter for some reason other than robbery, and the man who came along later and helped himself to Lassiter's money."

"He'd hide it in the woods somewhere," Wayne guessed. "Too risky for him to bring it into town."

"What a shame," Verna murmured, "that the Arkansas orphanage won't get it!"

"The orphanage," her uncle amended, "will at

least get whatever we can sell the ranch for. Lassiter was advertizing it for nine thousand, and as liquidator of the estate I'm re-advertizing it for the same price, in current issues of both the *Pilot* and the *Sentinel*."

The lawyer looked at a wall clock and stood up. "Time to eat. Verna and I are lunching at the Sheridan. Be glad to have you join us, young man."

The stagecoach from Wolcott was standing in front of the hotel when they got there, waiting for a new driver and fresh horses. Passengers booked through to Hahn's Peak were inside, eating. Bainbridge and his guests took a corner table.

Brady saw Dale Garrison eating alone across the room. The man caught Verna's eye and waved a hand. The smile she gave him had restraint in it. It was clear to Brady that she didn't quite trust the man, although she didn't yet know about the four quarterly deposits he'd made at the bank.

Should he tell her? He decided not to; best to wait till he had something more on Garrison than a ride he'd made to Bart Conroy's cabin on the murder day, plus four mysterious cash deposits.

Coach passengers got up and hurried out. Then from the street came wheel sounds as the stage left on its afternoon run to Hahn's Peak.

A waitress served the Bainbridge party, and

111

they'd almost finished when a man came into the dining room and went directly to Garrison's table. He didn't sit down, merely stood there for a minute in subdued conversation. The talk seemed to disturb Garrison. His normal, unruffled composure seemed, to Brady, to desert him for a moment. Then Garrison made a quick recovery, managed a smile, and spoke a few glib words himself. Apparently they satisfied the standing man, who turned and went out.

But not before Wayne Brady had seen who he was—a liveryman named Reinhart. It was at the Reinhart stable that Garrison had rented a saddle horse and been gone with it for about forty hours. A journey which he claimed had taken him no farther north than Bart Conroy's cabin.

Now that same liveryman had taken the trouble to walk to the hotel for a word with Garrison. Why?

Presently the Bainbridge party finished their coffee and left the dining room. At the lobby desk the lawyer paid the check, and while he was doing it Brady had time for a word aside with the girl.

"I never get to see you any more, Verna, since you quit living at the hotel. What about tonight? Could I drop up to the cottage for a while?"

"It will be nice to have you, Wayne. Eight o'clock?"

"On the dot." Wayne went only to the front walk with them. There he thanked the lawyer and then hurried on alone to the Reinhart stable.

"Saw you talking to Garrison at the hotel," he said bluntly to the liveryman. "What about? We've been checking up on that ride he made to Conroy's."

Reinhart took him to a saddle room and showed him an ordinary riding bridle. "It's the one we took off the horse we rented Garrison when he turned it in here," Reinhart said.

Brady looked curiously at the bridle. "What's wrong with it?"

"Nothing. But the bridle he left with had one rein which was about six inches shorter than the other. This bridle he came back with has reins of equal length, like they should be. Doesn't matter much; except it got to botherin' me a little on account of you and Jack Camp askin' me about that rental."

At once Brady was alert. "So a little while ago you braced him about it. What did he say?"

"He said the only place he off-saddled was at Conroy's, where he stayed all night. Said he must've picked up the wrong bridle when he saddled up to ride home the next day."

"Thanks. Please keep this under your hat, Mr. Reinhart, until we've checked on it."

Brady made fast time to the jail office and found Jack Camp there. The undersheriff listened to the bridle story and was impressed. "I doubt very much if Bart Conroy owns an extra bridle.

He'd ridden to the Cary ranch and was working there as a hay hand. He'd be forking his own saddle and using his own bridle. No chance for Garrison to pick up the wrong bridle if only one was there."

Brady followed up shrewdly. "But if Garrison rode on to the Lassiter ranch, he'd find Lassiter's horse in the corral, with Lassiter's saddle and bridle on the saddle tree at the front of the barn. Let's say he rode up about noon, unsaddled at the barn, walked to the house hoping to be invited to lunch—and instead found Lassiter dead. A note guides him to the money and he grabs it. Then in a sweat to get away, he saddles up in too big a hurry. Doesn't notice that he picks up the wrong bridle instead of the one he came with."

"If he did," Camp summed up, "the livery stable bridle is still there. If it is, it nails Garrison for a liar and goes a long way toward nailing him for a thief." The undersheriff frowned into space for a moment and then came to a decision. "Look, Brady. I've got to stay here in town and sit on the Bundchu case till Farnham gets back from the Peak. But I have authority to swear in an emergency deputy. What about letting me put a badge on you? A badge and a gun."

It didn't take Brady long to think it over. Without the authority of a deputyship he could hardly be more than a meddler. He was out to clear Jim Gentry and must prove that guilt lay

114

elsewhere. When he found the proof he'd need a badge in order to make an arrest.

"Swear me in, Jack." Brady held up his right hand.

A few minutes later he was wearing a badge, but declined Camp's offer of a gun. "I've got my own, Jack."

"Okay. Get an early start in the morning and ride up to Slater Park. You'll find Walt Cody there. My bet is you'll find something else—a bridle with one short rein in Lassiter's barn. Maybe by now Cody's come onto something. If he has, the two of you can run it down."

In his room at the Sheridan, Dale Garrison paced nervously. That damned bridle! The law was sure to check on it. They'd already checked once with Reinhart, and they'd no doubt check again. It wouldn't take them long to find out that Conroy had left no extra bridle in the shed back of his cabin. What they *would* find was a livery stable bridle in Lassiter's barn.

It still wouldn't prove he'd stolen the Lassiter money. Technically he hadn't—because the money was still under a well coping stone, where Lassiter himself had put it.

Then there was the matter of the four quarterly deposits. His explanation of them couldn't be disproved, but he was sure the law didn't believe it. Taken together with the bridle business, at the very least it would discredit Garrison and strip away his mask of respectability.

What he wanted was to get his hands on the Lassiter money, plus whatever he could pry out of Abner Barnett, and take off for San Francisco by way of Wyoming and the U.P.

There wasn't a chance in the world that he could ride secretly to Slater Park and slip up in darkness to the well coping cache. The law was watching him; they'd already searched his room. How else could they have found out about those quarterly deposits?

Also, he knew that they'd sent Walt Cody to the Lassiter ranch to act as watchdog there. In any case he'd need to rent a livery mount, and no doubt the livery people had been coached to report any such rental by Garrison.

Right now they didn't have enough on him to justify an arrest. If he made off empty-handed at once, they could hardly stop him. It was just a little more than a hundred miles to Rawlins, Wyoming, from which trains left daily for the Pacific coast.

How could he get to Rawlins? There was a regular stage line from here down the Yampa River to Craig, and from Craig another stage line which ran north to Rawlins via Baggs. The schedules were published in the local weeklies.

This week's *Sentinel* lay on the table, and Garrison picked it up for a look. Skimming through it for stage schedules, he saw an ad which had just been inserted by Nathan Bainbridge.

FOR SALE
IMPROVED SLATER PARK RANCH.

To liquidate the estate of the late Mark Lassiter, his 320-acre ranch in Slater Park is offered for immediate sale. Good house, stable, sheds, well, ditch, hay meadow. Price, $9000.00. Terms, $1000.00 down and balance at the end of probate, six months from now. See Nathan Bainbridge, Attorney. Immediate possession.

Almost at once Garrison saw a way out of his own tight corner. It would be a perfectly safe way to pick up the money now under the well coping and move on with it to catch a westbound train at Rawlins.

For all the past year he'd been masquerading as a prospective ranch buyer. Why not actually be one? Here was a ranch for sale which, for a down payment, he could occupy as legitimate owner. Why not make the down payment, move openly to the ranch, and as its resident master pick up the money and make off with it? He need never come back. He'd simply default on the balance due, allowing title to revert to the Lassiter estate.

To Garrison it seemed foolproof. Right now Walt Cody was living in the bunk cabin as watchman. But as owner Garrison would simply walk in on Cody and dismiss him. There'd be nothing that Cody, Brady, Camp, Bainbridge, or anyone else could do about it. After that Garrison could simply mark time, for weeks, months if necessary, till they got tired of watching him. He needn't touch the money till he was ready to ride north to Rawlins.

With the *Sentinel* advertizement in hand, Garrison went out and walked briskly to Nathan Bainbridge's office. Verna admitted him with an uncertain smile. "It's about this ad," Garrison told her. "Is your uncle busy?"

He wasn't. The girl ushered him into the lawyer's private office.

"Been scouting this county for a year," Garrison said, "for a good ranch property. Looked at maybe a dozen of 'em. Notice you're offering the Lassiter place for nine thousand."

Bainbridge nodded. "Yes, for the benefit of a nonresident heir. Final title can't be transferred until the estate goes through probate, which will take about six months. But possession can be had for a one-thousand dollar good faith payment and a mortgage note for the balance. Are you interested, Garrison?"

Garrison answered by bringing out a Milner bank checkbook. He wrote a check for one thousand dollars payable to the Lassiter estate and tossed it on the desk.

"I'm not only interested, I'm sold. Give me a receipt; you can make out the mortgage note and I'll sign it."

Bainbridge eyed him shrewdly. "You mean you're willing to buy the property sight-unseen?"

"Not sight-unseen," Garrison rejoined smoothly. "On one of my earliest scouting trips, about ten months ago, I passed by Slater Park and stopped overnight there. Lassiter showed me around, and I liked the looks of the place. That was before he had any thought of selling."

"Just before his death," Bainbridge reminded him, "he advertized the place. Why didn't you offer to buy it then?"

"I did. Saw him in town about a week before he died and offered him a thousand dollars down, balance on terms. He said no, he wanted at least half down. I couldn't raise that much, so nothing came of it."

Bainbridge picked up the check and gave it a quizzical stare. "First," he said finally, "I'll make sure this check's good. Next, I'll consult the sheriff and the county attorney to make sure you're not in any way complicated with the law. If you're not, I'll have no choice. I advertized the place on certain terms and you've met them. Drop in to see me day after tomorrow."

Garrison left the office, cautiously confident. Even if they found a short-rein bridle in Lassiter's barn, it wouldn't definitely prove he'd left it there himself. He'd deny it with his last breath. He'd insist that someone must have switched bridles on him. It would leave them with grounds for suspicion, but nothing more. In the end they'd have to accept his offer.

Anyway he'd know by this time day after tomorrow. And tonight he'd go calling. Not on Verna Bainbridge but on Abner Barnett.

X

Garrison waited till nightfall before making the call. The Barnett house was on Tenth Street, two blocks above Lincoln. A two-storey brick with an iron fence around the front lawn, it was easily the most imposing residence in Steamboat Springs.

This would be his fifth call here. Never once had Garrison set foot inside the Barnett store. Always he went to the house, and always after dark.

It was the only house in the block, and a flagged walk led from gate to porch. There was a porch lamp and a brass knocker. When Garrison knocked, the door was opened by Abner Barnett himself.

The town's leading merchant gave a disconcerted stare and made no move to step aside. "You're a month early," he protested.

"This," Garrison assured him blandly, "is not a collection call. Something's come up and I think you ought to know about it. Both you and . . ." he hesitated a moment before adding, ". . . shall we say Mrs. Barnett?"

A woman's voice called from the parlor. "Who is it, Abner?"

With a helpless shrug Barnett stepped aside and let Garrison into the hallway. From there they went into a tastefully decorated parlor where the lady of the house sat by a coffee cart. The Barnetts had just finished their after-dinner cups. She was a handsome woman, stylishly dressed and just under forty. Her shocked protest essentially echoed Barnett's.

"But it isn't time yet!"

"Not for nearly a month," Garrison agreed. He held out a hand. "If there's a cup of that coffee left, please, would you mind?"

Thelma Barnett minded, but she didn't dare rebuff him. She filled a cup and handed it to him. "You promised not to disturb us except on collection dates."

"This," Garrison explained, "is just to let you know that pretty soon—maybe in a couple of weeks or maybe in a couple of months—I'll be moving to the west coast. After that you'll never see me again. But you'll still send me the quarterly payments. When I get to the coast I'll let you know my address there. I don't even know myself yet."

The Barnetts exchanged looks of something

like vicarious relief. It would be better to have Garrison a thousand miles away than to have him on their doorstep. But the man's quick warning made their relief short-lived.

"It will be just as easy," he reminded them, "for me to send a letter from San Francisco to Hartford, Connecticut, as it is to send the same letter from Steamboat Springs. What I mean is— if any quarterly payment fails to arrive on the due date, I'll write and mail that letter."

This time the looks exchanged by the Barnetts were of bleak despair. Garrison's whip over them could strike from far as well as from near. Except for that dread, they had a solid position here, the most prosperous store in the county, a fine house and a high social standing. All would come tumbling down if Garrison cracked his whip.

"They'd get *you* too," Abner offered desperately, "the same as us."

"Not at all," Garrison countered. "I served my time, but you haven't."

They knew he'd spent three years in a New England prison for forgery, and on that charge his slate was wiped clean. "But what about extortion," Thelma Barnett challenged. "Bleeding us here in Colorado!"

"What about it?" Garrison said calmly. "If you accuse me, I'll deny it. Your word against mine. All payments were in cash, and will be. Not a

122

shred of proof you ever gave me a penny. Accusing me would only build up a case against yourselves."

Garrison sipped his coffee, then went on smoothly: "Not that it needs building up. Let's review it for a minute, Barnett. Four years ago, in 1897, you were a bachelor banker in Hartford. That was the year you made off with eighty thousand dollars of the bank's money, at the same time running away with a married woman. Each of you went by a different route to Denver. You met there. From Denver, travelling as Mr. and Mrs. Barnett, you rode a train to Wolcott and from there came by stagecoach to Steamboat Springs. It looked like a hiding place no one would ever find. The main general store was for sale and you bought it. As a smart business man you made it prosper and by 1900 it and other investments were netting you about $12,000 a year."

"And then," Barnett supplemented bitterly, "you came along."

"Yes—I came along. And it happened like this. Getting out of prison in 1900, I headed west where nobody knew me. I was about to settle in Denver when a party of Boston capitalists checked into my hotel, on the lookout for mining investments. One of them knew me by sight, so I figured I wasn't far enough west. Bought a ticket to Salt Lake City, and just at sundown my train made a supper stop at Wolcott, Colorado. That's where I spotted you, Wilcox. I didn't know then that you'd changed your name to Barnett.

"You were about to board a stagecoach. The name on the coach was 'Wolcott; Steamboat Springs and Hahn's Peak Stage Line.' The last passenger to get on had a vaguely familiar look. I asked a man on the walk, 'Who is that big guy with a beard?' He said, 'You mean Mr. Barnett? He's got a general store at Steamboat Springs; came over here to receive a shipment of goods and have it hauled by wagon over the range.'

" 'Steamboat Springs?' I asked. 'Where's that?'

" 'Other side of the divide in Routt County,' the man said."

Thinking back, Garrison remembered how he'd almost muffed it. His conductor had shouted "All aboard" and he'd got back on the train. The train was gliding down the Eagle River toward Glenwood Springs when he remembered. That vaguely familiar face at Wolcott! The sensational scandal three years ago! A Connecticut banker named Wilcox decamping with eighty thousand dollars—and the disappearance, at the same time, of a Boston society woman named Mrs. Clara St. Charles. Neither had been heard of since. Garrison had known Wilcox by sight, and in fact had once successfully forged a check on his Hartford bank.

Now he finished his coffee and set the cup

aside. "So I got off at the next station, Eagle," he resumed, "and rode an eastbound train back to Wolcott. Caught the next stage to Steamboat and put up at the Sheridan. Spent a week looking you over before I was sure."

He hadn't walked in on Barnett at the store. He'd called after dark at this Tenth Street residence, just like tonight. He remembered his bombshell greeting. "Mr. Wilcox of Hartford, I believe?"

First dismay, then panic, had chased the ruddiness from the merchant's face. "Who," he'd gasped, "are you?"

"Your new partner, Mr. Wilcox. Or Mr. Barnett, if you prefer. I'm pretty good at keeping my mouth shut, so don't worry. By the way, where is Mrs. St. Charles? Is she around somewhere?" He knew she was around because twice during the week he'd seen her on the street.

"Just what do you want?" Barnett had pled desperately.

"A fair cut of whatever you've got, Mr. Wilcox. Shall we talk it over?"

There'd been a long painful talk before they'd settled on terms. Barnett had no large amount of ready cash. His fortune was invested in his store, its stock, his residence, and a half interest in the local milling company. Finally Garrison had laid down an ultimatum. "Let's say it brings you in a net income of $12,000 a year. All I want is a

125

third—say a thousand dollars per quarter. If I don't get it I send two telegrams: one to a Connecticut sheriff, the other to the husband of the woman you ran away with."

Barnett's only choice had been surrender.

"I'm not upping the take any," Garrison assured him now. "The fifth quarterly payment's due next month. If I'm still in the county I'll call for it as usual. But if I'm gone by then, I'll notify you where to send the due payment. Have I made myself clear?"

He'd made himself clear—as clear as the gray helplessness on the man's face and the tears of despair in the woman's eyes.

Garrison got up and moved toward the door. There he turned with a slight bow. "Thank you for the coffee, Mrs. St. Charles."

Two blocks east in a cottage on upper Eighth Street, Wayne Brady was calling on Verna Bainbridge. The little parlor had bright new curtains and lamp shades. In the few days she'd been here, Verna had transformed a musty bachelor's quarters into a home.

"I'll be saddling up for Slater Park at daybreak," Brady said. "No tellin' when I'll get back."

"I can hardly believe it!" Verna exclaimed. "Mr. Garrison seemed such a nice man. Do they really think he stole Mr. Lassiter's money?"

"We'll keep our fingers crossed on it," Brady hedged, "until we check up on that bridle. Your uncle and Jack Camp and I were in a huddle over it all afternoon. Trying to figure out whether we oughta let Garrison buy that ranch and move on it."

"What did you finally decide?"

"We'll leave it up to Farnham and the county attorney. They're due in from the Peak on tomorrow's stage."

"What do *you* think they ought to do, Wayne?"

He'd given it a good deal of thought and had talked it over with Jim Gentry. Jim was going along with him in the morning on the ride to Slater Park. If a short-reined bridle was found in the barn there, Jim could return to Steamboat Springs with it while Brady remained up there with Walt Cody, awaiting further orders.

"My guess is," Brady said cautiously, "that Garrison picked up the Lassiter money but was afraid to bring it into town. It would be too hot to handle—with Lassiter dead in the ranch house. So he likely hid the money a little way off in the woods and came home empty-handed. He figured to slip up there when things cool down and dig up the money. He can't do that because we're watching him and he knows it. But if he owns the ranch and is living on it, it oughta be simple. Take him less than an hour any dark night to get his hands on the money again."

"Then we shouldn't let him buy the ranch, should we?"

"Camp thinks we shouldn't. I think we should—but at the same time keep an eye on him. Only way to get the deadwood on him'd be to catch him with the money in hand."

"But if it's his ranch, how can anyone stay there to watch without his permission?"

"Because, Verna, it'll still be the scene of an unsolved murder. That's why we've got Cody up there now. The law can keep Cody, or me, or any other deputy, on the lookout there indefinitely until we find out who killed Lassiter."

The voice of Nathan Bainbridge spoke from a doorway. "Exactly the recommendation I'll make to the county attorney tomorrow—whether or not we find the wrong bridle in the barn. There's a good bunk cabin, Jim Gentry tells us. We can let Garrison occupy the main house, as its lord and master, while you and Walt Cody bed down in the bunk cabin. Working two shifts, you can watch every move he makes."

"But Uncle Nathan," Verna intervened, "on those terms he'll withdraw his offer to buy, won't he?"

"Maybe. Maybe not. If he does it'll prove his offer wasn't sincere in the first place. Either way we checkmate him on digging up the money."

The mantel clock struck eleven and Wayne got up to go. "Have to be in the saddle by daylight.

128

Soon as we get there and look in the barn, I'll send Jim back with a report. So long, Mr. Bainbridge. I'll be looking you up, Verna, soon as I hit town again."

She went with him to the porch door, where he took his time saying goodnight. There was a porch lamp, and the mellow glow of it made the girl's face inviting and beautiful. Wayne Brady had an almost overpowering desire to take it between his hands and kiss her lips. Next time maybe he would. All he could do right now was say good-night.

After he'd said it twice, and three times, he turned reluctantly away. Verna still stood in the open door. It was then that the shot came—a gunshot from not more than ten paces to the left beyond the leftmost porch railing. Its bullet plowed down Wayne Brady's scalp and dropped him stunned to the porch floor.

XI

He wasn't out much more than ten minutes. When he came to, he was on a couch in the Bainbridge parlor with Verna and her uncle giving first aid. For a little while his only awareness was a throbbing at the top of his head. It was like someone had bludgeoned him with a club rather than with a bullet. Verna said softly: "We've sent for Doctor Solandt. Don't move, please."

But he wanted to move. As his head cleared he wanted to get up and give chase to whoever had fired the shot. "He was at the end of the porch," Bainbridge explained presently, "screened by a vine there and waiting for you to come out. We heard him running along the side of the house to the backyard and on toward the next street east. It was pitch dark, and the whole town had gone to bed. Not much chance that anyone saw him. . . . I think that'll be Doctor Solandt." Buggy wheels could be heard stopping in front.

Doctor Solandt came in with his medical bag and went briskly to work. "Only a scalp crease," he reported, "less than skin deep. They can feel like a sledgehammer, though, when they hit you that way."

He shaved off a narrow lane of hair and put on a patch. "Stay quiet for a day or two," he ordered cheerfully, "and you'll be as good as new."

By then Town Marshal Burgess had come in as well as a neighbor or two who'd heard the shot. Burgess listened to reports and then organized what was likely to be a futile chase through darkness.

Neither Verna, standing in the open doorway, nor Brady, turning away from her with hat in hand, had seen the sniper or even the flash of his gun. "That porch light made you a pretty fair target," Burgess said. "Range was less than ten steps. You're lucky to be alive, boy."

"It wasn't a rifle shot," Bainbridge was sure. "By its sound it was a pistol shot, fired by someone crouched just back of the end railing of the porch. No telling how long he'd been waiting there. The same gun, I'll wager, that fired through a window at Lassiter. And the same hand that struck down both Yancy and Bundchu."

Verna wanted Wayne kept at the cottage all night, but Solandt said it wasn't necessary. "I might as well take him to the hotel in my buggy and put him to bed in his own room."

Bainbridge added: "Your ride to Slater Park's off for a couple of days, Brady. We'll send Jim Gentry up there alone to check on that bridle. Now forget everything and get some rest."

He helped Solandt take Wayne out to the buggy, and the three drove down to the Sheridan Hotel. By then Wayne could think clearly, and as they crossed the lobby he suggested, "Let's find out when Garrison got in."

Garrison, they learned from the night clerk, had come in at half past ten and had idled in the lobby until after eleven. "Which puts him in the clear," Bainbridge concluded. The shot had been fired at exactly five minutes after eleven.

Wayne wasn't surprised. Garrison had never sized up as a gunman.

On the other hand, he could think of no one else with a motive strong enough to make him unloose a bullet meant to kill. The reason suggested by Bainbridge, that Bundchu's killer might think that Brady could identify him, didn't seem convincing. You can't identify a man when your only contact with him has been a clinch in the dark. And if Brady could point a finger at the man, why hadn't he already done so? A full day had passed since the clinch in the dark, over the dead or dying body of Otto Bundchu.

After they'd put him to bed and Solandt had given him an opiate, Wayne went quickly to sleep. His door was locked, and for tonight they'd posted a guard in the hall. Wayne wakened at daylight with sunlight on his window and the head pain almost entirely gone. Harry Monson, the hotel manager, knocked and offered to send up a breakfast tray.

Wayne wouldn't hear of it. He got up, bathed, shaved, dressed, and went down to the dining room. There he found Verna and her uncle, together with Undersheriff Camp, waiting to have a word with him. They took a table for four, and Wayne said impatiently: "Please stop babying me. I don't even have a headache any more. Give me another couple of hours, and I can hit the saddle for Slater Park."

"Jim Gentry," Camp told him, "is already on his way there. Rest of us 'll stand pat here till he gets back with or without that livery stable bridle."

"We've dug the bullet," Bainbridge said, "out of

a porch post. A forty-five calibre slug—just like the one that killed Lassiter. Fresh bootprints beyond the porch railing where the shot came from."

Verna gave a shiver. "An inch lower and it would have killed you too, Wayne. When you dropped on the porch, right in front of me, I thought you were dead until . . ."

Wayne looked at her curiously. "Until what, Verna?"

"Until I kneeled by you and heard you give a moan of pain. Then I knew . . ."

"Wait a minute," Wayne cut in. "That reminds me of something. Something that happened when I was clinching with the killer in Room 209."

"Yes?" Bainbridge prompted alertly. "Go on."

"It was pitch black," Wayne reminded them. "Bundchu was on the floor, dead or dying. The killer was somewhere in the room, stalking me, groping toward me, ready to give me the same treatment. He wasn't going to let me get out of that room if he could help it. And I knew it. So ninety-nine percent of my attention was on him. I had no time to think about a man on the floor."

"But you remember something now?" the lawyer coaxed.

"Only vaguely. And it was only what seemed to be a moan of pain from Bundchu. Probably the last sound he made before he died. It sounded like 'Oh!' Just a one-syllable moan or groan. Oh!

It came just about the time I clinched with the killer, and I didn't think of it again till just now."

"You sock a man hard," Jack Camp put in, "and he'll more'n likely give out a sound like that. So what?"

"So right now I'm wondering," Wayne brooded. "Maybe it wasn't a moan of pain. Maybe it was a name. A one-syllable name with a long O sound: like Joe, for instance. Maybe he was trying to tell me who whanged down on him."

Camp gave an open-mouthed stare. "You mean we oughta start lookin' for a guy named Joe?"

"Joe or some other short name with an 'O' sound. And if I'm right, it could explain something which didn't make any sense before."

Nathan Bainbridge gave him a keen look. "What didn't make sense before, son?"

"The man's reason for gunning me last night. The reason you gave me, Mr. Bainbridge, won't stand up very well. It has to be something more than that—like if his name's Joe, for instance."

The lawyer's eyes narrowed shrewdly. "Maybe you've got something," he admitted. "Whatever Bundchu said with his last breath was heard by the killer as well as by you. To you it meant nothing at the moment except perhaps a moan of pain. But to the killer it could mean his name—and his neck! Your mind was on the killer, but we can be sure a good part of the killer's mind was on Bundchu. Wondering if he was still alive;

wondering if he'd name his assailant. If he did, and you heard correctly, it would make you as dangerous to him as Bundchu."

The undersheriff got grimly to his feet. "I've heard enough. Anyway it's the only lead we've got. I'm off for Brooklyn to find out how many Joes they've got over there."

In midmorning Doctor Solandt examined Brady's head. "This time tomorrow you can kick up your heels, boy. Meantime just take it easy and keep out of trouble."

The noon stage brought Sheriff Farnham and County Attorney Gray from Hahn's Peak. Wayne Brady didn't see them but late in the day Jack Camp came by with a report.

"Four or five Joes over at Saloon Row, but they've all got alibis for eleven o'clock last night. Not very reliable alibis, but it's likely we can't shake 'em. A dozen or so more Joes here on the respectable side of the river, but none of 'em seem to fit our case. Maybe it was just a moan of pain after all."

"Maybe," Wayne admitted. "But it's the only thing that explains why the man wrote my name on a bullet. He had to have a solid-reason, taking a chance like that. What did Gray and Farnham say?"

"Bainbridge recommended that we play along with Garrison like you suggest: sell him the ranch and let him occupy it—but post a tight watch in the bunk cabin. A two-shift watch by you and Walt Cody. Gray says the bridle evidence by itself will be too thin and circumstantial; says we can't convict Garrison unless we nab him with the goods. Garrison'll claim someone switched bridles on him, and we can't positively prove it isn't true."

Wayne had an easy night, and by ten the next morning Jim Gentry was back from Slater Park. The bridle he brought with him had one rein which was six inches shorter than the other. Reinhart definitely identified it as belonging to his stable. Confronted with it, Dale Garrison stood pat. "If somebody left that bridle in Lassiter's barn, it wasn't me. I never went an inch farther north than Conroy's."

"You still want to buy the Slater Park ranch?" Farnham asked him.

"Why not? Soon as Bainbridge says the word I'll head that way with a cook and a packload of grub."

"Fair enough, Garrison. But mind you, we're still investigating Lassiter's murder. So for the time being we'll keep a man or two in the bunk cabin. If you want possession on those terms you can have it."

If the man was taken aback, he didn't show it. "It's okay with me. I've nothing to hide. I'd better go tell Tom to start getting ready."

Indian Tom, they knew, was a halfbreed Ute cook who sometimes worked on ranches, sometimes for Steamboat Springs restaurants, sometimes as a hunting guide. He knew the forests of Routt County as well as anyone. Garrison had lured him with top pay and before the day ended had used his advice to buy two saddle horses and a pack mare. Brady saw them loading up with supplies in front of the Adair store.

"Looks like he really means it," Town Marshal Burgess remarked.

"He's not the kind," Wayne said, "who'd hole up in the woods all by himself. He's used to being waited on. A townie, if I ever saw one. And if he needs a guide in order to make a fast fadeout by night, after he picks up the money, Indian Tom'd be just the man for him."

Nothing else happened that day. Jim Gentry went back to Brooklyn to resume his watch there. At the next noon Wayne idled on the hotel walk to see the stage from Wolcott roll in. Passengers got off and went in to eat. A few local people got on with tickets to Hahn's Peak. One of them was a Steamboat Springs man known to Wayne by sight and reputation—a mining expert named Ambrose Kincaid: a tall, personable man with a Van Dyke beard whose professional card ran in both the Routt County weeklies. Wayne was aware that he made his living as a broker of mining properties and as a consultant. A good

137

deal of his time was spent in the Hahn's Peak district, although his office was here in Steamboat.

Since his name wasn't Joe, or anything that rhymed with Joe, he was of no particular interest to Brady. The man was sitting up top with Driver Marshman when the stage rolled out for the Peak.

XII

Ambrose Kincaid arrived at Hahn's Peak in time for supper at the Larson Hotel. There was room for him, for the district court session was over and most of the lawyers, litigants, and witnesses were now gone. Kincaid was a familiar figure here and more than once had brought along non-resident investors to look at mining properties. His opinion on mineral values was respected and widely sought. Mrs. Larson considered him a star customer, always giving him her best space and service.

"What brings you to us this time, Mr. Kincaid?"

"The usual, Mrs. Larson. A look here and a look there. Clients are always asking what's going on up here; so I have to keep myself posted."

The woman sighed. "We're getting deader every day, I'm afraid." She knew, as did everyone else at the Peak, that Kincaid kept a saddle mule and a blanket roll at the Hahn's Peak stage and livery barn. They were always ready for him when he needed to ride out to some place like Whisky Park or Way's Gulch or Columbine. She knew too that he owned stock in the area's three most important mines—the *Minnie D*, the *Elkhorn*, and the *Tom Thum*.

After supper Kincaid walked up the camp's dark dusty street to the stage barn and made sure that his mule was in the corral there. "Grain him," he told the barnman, "and stall him for the night with a mangerful of bright hay. Right after breakfast I'll be taking a ride upcountry."

"He'll be ready, Mr. Kincaid."

On the way back to the hotel he stopped at the Peak's one shabby saloon. Ten years ago it had been Big John's place, but with the decline of the district Big John had moved to his stand across the river from Steamboat Springs. Tonight only four or five bewhiskered customers were on hand. Kincaid waved them to the bar and stood treat.

It paid to keep himself popular here.

A wizened Chinese bartender served them. All took whisky except Kincaid, who took sherry wine. He'd abstained from hard liquor since leaving Arizona many years ago. "By the way," he inquired presently, "are the Pomeroy brothers still over in Way's Gulch?"

A miner snickered. "They sure are, Mr. Kincaid. And why anyone 'd want to stick to that played-out strip of gravel beats me. Gold's gettin' about as scarce over there as whisky."

"Dry as a camel's gullet," another man agreed.

Way's Gulch lay just two miles southeast over a low, timbered ridge. In the early days it had been the district's main camp and post office. Captain Way himself, who in the Sixties with Joseph Hahn and Bill Doyle had discovered this gold area, had parcelled out the cabin plots in Way's Gulch with the strict provision that no liquor could ever be sold there. And none ever had been. For thirty-three years the Way's Gulch miners had had to walk two miles through the forest to Hahn's Peak whenever they wanted a drink.

Only a few were left there now. Of those few, two were Hank and Frank Pomeroy, blizzard-bit old-timers, both of them, but as deeply religious and abstemious as had been Captain Way himself. Ambrose Kincaid knew that about them— and one thing more; the Pomeroy brothers were scrupulously honest.

Their sterling integrity made them important to his plan. He needed a pair of experienced and rugged miners who wouldn't steal from him, whatever the opportunity, and none could fit that specification so well as the Pomeroys.

Having made sure that they were still grubbing away over at Way's Gulch, Kincaid went to the hotel and to bed.

In the morning he got an early start. A bedroll

was tied back of his saddle cantle, although he was hoping not to stay out overnight. Often in the past he'd camped out, sometimes for as long as a week, in wildernesses like the Farwell Mountain district or Hog Park. A short-barreled carbine was in his saddle scabbard, and his bedroll had a six-gun. It was a rough country full of rough men.

Yet in all the time he'd been in Routt County Kincaid had never used the rifle except for camp meat, nor the six-gun for defense against hold-up men. Using it for defense against exposure was something else. Four potential exposers had crossed his path—Lassiter, Yancy, Bundchu, and Brady. He knew not that he'd gone off half-cocked in the case of Brady. If that nosey cowboy really knew anything, or had heard anything in Room 209, he'd have spilled it to the law by this time.

The main items in his bedroll were a short-handled shovel, a crude sluice pan, four small pine stakes, and four empty bean cans. These he'd carried around with him for years in case he should suddenly want to test and stake a mining claim.

In his pocket was a pad of blank filing forms.

He jogged his mule up the Columbine trail, but presently left it and turned up Willow Creek. Making sure that no one was within sight, he guided his mule northwesterly toward a towering pinnacle landmark known as the Nipple. Much of the time he was in timber and could see only a short way ahead. He'd never before had occasion to ride this way. All pay strikes of the district had been in other directions; everything to the west of Hahn's Peak had long ago been ruled out as barren country as far as mineral prospects were concerned.

From an inner pocket he took the rough sketch given him by Otto Bundchu. It showed that Oliver Creek headed about a mile south of the Nipple. Kincaid had often studied a Routt County map and knew roughly the course of Oliver Creek—a small, unimportant stream high in the forest and meandering northwesterly to join the South Fork of the Little Snake.

The weight of his bedroll kept the mule at a slow walk, and Kincaid had been asaddle nearly two hours when he crossed a wooded divide and dropped down into a watershed which slanted westerly. With the high landmark of the Nipple only about a mile off to the right he knew that the tiny stream of water here had to be the head of Oliver Creek.

In the next mile the run doubled in size as feeders came in from left and right. Kincaid followed down the north bank of it, watching alertly for a lightning-struck lodgepole pine snag. Sooner than he expected, he came to it. And just as described by Bundchu, there was a knothole about eight feet above the ground.

This far, at least, Bundchu's directions were

verified. Exactly as Bundchu had advised, Kincaid stood on the saddle of his mule to reach a hand into the knothole. His fingers touched rusty tin. What he brought out was a bean can with a scrap of paper in it. In faded and barely legible writing on the paper was the name Bundchu.

The snag stood about thirty paces from the creeklet. The flow of water here was only about the size of a man's body, but in seasons of melting snow it would be considerably more. Through winter months this entire upper watershed would be perhaps five or six feet deep in snow.

Kincaid rode downstream a little more than a quarter of a mile and came to an outcrop of red sandstone—just as specified by Bundchu. Here then was almost surely the Karl Janvers gulch, from which Janvers, working alone, had panned more than thirty thousand dollars in gold during four short summers—and where he'd been shot dead by Bundchu.

Riding about halfway back to the snag, Kincaid took the bedroll from his mule and opened it to get a short shovel and a gravel pan. The creeklet showed no signs of having been worked. Naturally it wouldn't. Summer freshets and ten winters of deep snow would blot out all sign of the Janvers operation. And for Kincaid, a mining expert, an hour or two of testing should prove or disprove the presence of pay gravel here.

Kneeling by the water, he was soon at it, filling

his pan, whirling it, rocking it, draining off the water to inspect the sandy sediment left. A sluice trough with cleats would be more efficient, but this would do for a few rough tests. His first several pans showed no color. He dipped deeper, then tried again fifty yards up the run.

Here his second dip showed gleams of yellow. His next brought up a gold nugget, pea-size. A bigger one came with his next dip. He used the shovel to gouge deeper into the gravel. Another show of color. For a busy hour more he whirled and rocked his pan. First upstream, then downstream. In all it brought him perhaps two ounces of dust and nuggets.

About thirty-five dollars worth! Enough to be more than convincing. Beyond any reasonable doubt this was the place! Here was the long-lost Karl Janvers placer bonanza!

The job now was to stake and file it. What he really needed to file would be a placer claim—forty acres by Colorado law. But to do that he'd have to know the exact subdivision of section, township, and range. His county map told him that he was in Township 10 North, Range 86 West. It showed that the head of Oliver Creek was just a little way below the north line of that township and about halfway between range lines, so he was probably in either Section 3 or Section 4.

That wouldn't be close enough for a legal placer description. So he decided to file a lode claim, which would be a rectangle five hundred by two hundred yards, and whose boundaries wouldn't need to follow government land lines. That would effectively hold title for the time being. Later, after engaging Land Commissioner Wintersteen of Steamboat Springs to locate a section corner near the filing, either he or his assignee if need be could file an overlapping placer claim.

He took his four wooden stakes, his four empty bean cans, and a pad of filing blanks up to the lightning-struck lodgepole pine snag. Using a rock as a hammer, he drove one of the stakes near the base of the snag. Then he filled out a filing blank, using lode claim dimensions.

On the first line he wrote his name. The next line was for the name of the claim. Bundchu had demanded that he use the name "Little Joe"— actually the name of a bartender twenty years ago at the Wyatt Earp saloon in Tombstone, Arizona, and now a lifer in the Colorado penitentiary. Of all the names in the language that would be the last which Kincaid would want to use.

The name he wrote on the blank was "The *Flamingo*."

The description he wrote read in part: "Beginning at a stone monument thirty-two paces north of Oliver Creek and twelve paces north of a lightning-struck lodgepole pine snag, and just south of the north line of Section . . ." he left the section number blank for the time being ". . . Township 10 North, Range 86 West, Routt County, Colorado, thence five hundred yards westerly and paralleling said Oliver Creek to a wooden stake near an outcrop of red sandstone; thence two hundred yards southerly, thence five hundred yards easterly, thence two hundred yards northerly to the point of beginning."

It took nearly an hour, patiently writing, to make five copies. Kincaid put one copy in his pocket for filing tomorrow at the county clerk's office. The second copy he put in a tin can and inverted the can over his stake. Next he made a pile of stones two feet high near the stake. It would do for a monument.

With three stakes and three cans he paced five hundred yards westerly, paralleling the creek. There he drove another stake and over it inverted another can with a copy of his filing notice in it. He then paced southerly two hundred yards, crossing the creek, to the southwest corner of his rectangle. There he drove a third stake and put a can over it. Then he paced five hundred yards east, where he staked the fourth and last corner.

With all corners staked and labeled, he went back to his mule. By then it was late afternoon. He was headily sure that the Janvers gulch was now his own.

But as he rode slowly back toward Hahn's Peak, he knew quite well that sluicepan strikes can be short-lived and fickle. The Oliver Creek water run was perhaps too small to yield pay-sand for more than a few short seasons. In winter it would be snowed under. And maybe Janvers had already skimmed the cream from it.

In any case Ambrose Kincaid had no thought of working it himself. He knew of a better way, a safer way, a faster way to capitalize on the claim.

When County Clerk Withers opened his office in the morning, Kincaid was waiting at the door. "Want to take a look at your record books, Mr. Withers. Give me the volume that shows Township 10 North, Range 86 West."

The county clerk raised an eyebrow. "Nothing much over that way but pine woods and sheep range. You going into the sheep business, Kincaid?"

"I hope not. Mining's about all I know and I'd better stick to it."

Withers brought a heavy volume, ledger-size, from his safe and put it on a table. Kincaid sat down in front of it. Each of the long, wide pages was checkerboarded into thirty-six squares, each square representing a numbered section of land. Kincaid flipped pages until he found one headed T 10 N; R 86 W.

It showed that a few homesteaded quarter sections had been filed near the southeast corner of the township. The north end of the township was mostly unfiled wilderness. Blue lines were creek lines—Willow Creek, Lopez Creek, Larson Creek, Floyd Creek, Oliver Creek. Kincaid's only attention was to Oliver Creek. It was shown heading in Section 4, from there passing westerly through Sections 3 and 2.

After a close scrutiny Kincaid concluded that his *Flamingo* filing was in Section 3. He took from his pocket the claim blank he'd filled out yesterday and wrote "three" after the word section. Then he handed the paper to Clerk Withers. "Put this on record for me, please."

He handed over the filing fee and took a receipt. The county clerk looked quizzically at the description. "Out west of here, huh? Never heard of any strikes over that way."

"Just a hunch of mine," Kincaid said. He watched Withers put his stamp and seal on the filing, then left the office.

At the barn he saddled his mule and rode two miles southeast through the woods to Way's Gulch. Only a few of the old placer claims there were still being worked; and most of its shabby little cabins were unoccupied. One still in use housed the Pomeroy brothers, Hank and Frank.

Hank was big; Frank was small; both were shaggy and work-worn. They'd come in over the divide thirty-three years ago with Hahn and Way and Doyle. Both were still under sixty, toughened by rugged winters, hard-muscled after thirty summers of wielding picks and shovels.

When they took Kincaid into their cabin, he saw an open Bible on the table there. Hank poured coffee. "What's on your mind, Mr. Kincaid?"

"I've filed a gold claim," he told them, "and haven't got time or energy to work it myself. So I'll make you a proposition. I'll pay you ten dollars a day each to work it for me for the next thirty days; or if you prefer you can work it on shares, you take half of whatever you pan out and I'll take the other half. If you like what you find there, you can each file an adjacent claim for yourselves. Day pay or shares, take your choice."

To the brothers it sounded like a windfall. Twenty dollars a day was more than Way's Gulch had netted them for years.

"Where is this claim?" Hank asked eagerly.

"Only about eight miles from the Peak. I can take you there right now, and you can be back home by dark. You can pan a few dips and decide whether you want day pay or shares."

Hank looked at his brother. "What have we got to lose, Frank?"

Two hours later three men were riding west out of Hahn's Peak—Kincaid on his mule and the Pomeroys on rented livery mounts. The brothers had panning equipment with them. After an hour's testing, Kincaid promised, they'd be ready to make a choice between day pay or shares.

Just after midday they came to Oliver Creek. Hank gave it a skeptical look and said with a grimace: "Don't look like a pay gulch to me, Mr. Kincaid. Not enough water; and it's in the wrong part of the country."

"Try it and see," Kincaid suggested.

He removed the tin can from his monument stake, took out the filing notice, and wrote on it the word "three" after "Section."

As the brothers made ready for some panning tests, Kincaid walked three hundred yards west to the second corner stake. There he again wrote the word "three" in the blank space he'd left on the filing paper. Leisurely he visited the other two claim corners and amended the papers there in the same way.

By the time he rejoined the Pomeroys he could tell by their excited faces that each of them had found color.

At the end of two hours testing they came to him with open hands. Hank's cupped hand had about an ounce of gold dust in it. Frank's had half an ounce plus a pea-size nugget. "Altogether," Frank reported jubilantly, "it comes to about thirty dollars. More 'n we made all last week over at our gulch. We didn't even work up a sweat either."

Hank said: "We'll take the share deal, Mr. Kincaid, if it's all right with you."

"It's yours for thirty days," Kincaid agreed. "After that you can work adjacent claims of your own, if you care to stake them. Meantime let's keep our mouths shut and our gold out of sight."

"A good idea," Frank said. "No use startin' a stampede over this way; not till we get all snug and settled."

As they rode back toward Hahn's Peak, Kincaid promised them something else. "There's a cabin builder down at Steamboat Springs who'll build a forest cabin anywhere in the county for eight hundred dollars. A two-room cabin with log walls, a plank floor, two windows, and one door. I'll have him build a cabin at my expense on the *Flamingo*. You can live in it if you like, whether you work your own claims or mine."

"Fine!" Frank exclaimed. "We'll take a pack outfit and a tent over there and camp out till the cabin gets finished. It's a good deer country. With a cabin and a sack of flour we could hole up there all winter."

"I'll take the morning stage to Steamboat," Kincaid told them. "Be back in a few days with that cabin contractor."

When they dismounted at the Hahn's Peak barn, Frank said: "Here's the first divvy, Mr. Kincaid." He was holding out a hand with a generous ounce of gold dust in it—half of what their test pans had brought today.

Kincaid accepted it without comment. It was the last proof he needed that these two men would never let him down.

XIII

"A phony if I ever saw one!" Walt Cody snorted, and Wayne Brady agreed with him. They were sitting on the bunk cabin steps at the Slater Park ranch.

Eighty yards away, in the corral, Dale Garrison set astride a horse with a lariat in hand. He whirled the loop around his head, then tossed it at the corral's snubbing post. Missing widely, he pulled in his rope and tried again.

He'd been here four days now, with Indian Tom cooking for him at the main house.

Generally he slept till midmorning, then spent the rest of the day striding or riding around the premises in corduroys, cowman's hat, and spurred boots.

"Claims he's waitin' for a Bob Baxter," Cody derided. "For my money, there ain't any Bob Baxter."

"You'd win your bet," Brady agreed. "I figure it's just a name he dreamed up to explain why he's killing time here. What he's really waiting for is for us to get tired watchin' him and pull out. Long as we're here he doesn't dare lay a hand on that Lassiter money."

A sincere ranch buyer, Brady reasoned, would be busily engaged in equipping and stocking the place. "But he knows we know that, Walt, so he hands us this line about Baxter."

Baxter, according to Garrison, was an experienced cattle hand who'd been a boyhood friend of Garrison's down in New Orleans. Years ago Baxter had come west and spent a few seasons cowboying around Wyoming and Colorado. Later Garrison had run into him at Denver and mentioned his plan to buy a western stock ranch. "And when I get one, Bob, I'll need your help running it."

"Nothin' I'd like better, pal. Just whistle when you want me," Baxter had replied.

That was the Baxter story and Garrison was sticking to it.

"It's like all the rest of his stories," Brady said. "You don't believe 'em but you can't prove they're not true. Like his song and dance about how he gets a thousand dollars every three months."

They watched Garrison miss the snubbing post a few more times and then finally ring it with a loop. After that the man unsaddled, left his mount in the corral, and came out into the ranchyard. Spotting Wayne and Walt on the bunk cabin steps, he came brazenly to them.

"I sure wish old Bax'd show up," he complained. "I wrote him where to come—and I sure need his advice."

"About what?" Brady asked.

"Lots of things. First of all, about how and

when to stock up. Should I stock up now or wait till spring? Should I run he-stuff or breeding stuff? What would you do in my place, Brady?"

Basically it was a fair question, and Wayne Brady, a stock lover, gave it a fair answer. "I wouldn't run breeding stuff. Not the year around at this altitude." The Slater Park altitude was nearly eight thousand feet. "Too much snow in the early spring when calves are dropping. You'd have better luck buying steer calves and holding them till they make beef. That's what Lassiter did."

"A better way yet," Cody put in, "would be to run this place in cahoots with some low-altitude ranch down on the Yampa. Both outfits could summer their stuff up here where the mountain grass grows high and winter it down where the snow's not so danged deep."

"Thanks," Garrison said. "I'll see what Bax thinks about that. If he doesn't show up in a day or two, guess I'll ride down to Steamboat and see if there's a letter from him."

Brady cocked an eye. "Did this Baxter fella ever tell you what outfits he's worked for?"

"Seems to me he did." Garrison wrinkled his brow and appeared to be concentrating. "Yeh, he mentioned a big cowman named Ora Haley up around Laramie, Wyoming."

Wayne and Walt exchanged looks. In cattle circles Ora Haley was a name to conjure with.

His vast herds ran on two ranges: one along the Little Laramie River in Wyoming; the other in Brown's Park in the western end of this Colorado county. Hundreds of cowboys, at one time or another, had been on his payroll.

"You men picked up any clews yet?" Garrison asked idly. "I mean about who shot Lassiter."

Brady grimaced and shook his head. "But we keep looking. Sheriff told us not to give up; told us to stick right here till we turn up some dead-wood. You gotta have patience, the sheriff says. You never know when somethin'll turn up."

"Or when somethin'll get dug up," Walt added slyly.

Garrison pretended to miss his meaning. It wasn't the first time Cody had baited him, and he was steeled against it. Up at the main house Indian Tom appeared and beat on a gong. "Mess time," Garrison said. "You men like to join me? Tom knocked over some sage chickens and there'll be more'n I can eat."

"No thanks." Brady waved him away, and they watched the man walk to the house, spurs jingling.

"All he needs," Walt exploded, "is batwing chaps and crossed gunbelts."

"And a foreman named Baxter," Brady added. "I'd better ask the sheriff to write Ora Haley and find out if Ora ever hired anyone by that name."

"What do we do if Garrison rides to Steamboat for his mail?"

"I'll have to ride along with him," Brady decided. "We don't dare let him get out of our sight in the woods. He might dig up the Lassiter money and hit for parts unknown."

It was a battle of wits—a waiting game which could turn out to be a stalemate. Chances were ten to one that Garrison's down payment on the ranch was merely an excuse to occupy it, and that he planned to desert it the minute he got his hands on hidden loot.

"Time's on his side, Walt. He knows we can't stay here forever. I'm on a deputy's pay and you're on watchman's pay. The taxpayers wouldn't stand for it if we run up too big a bill on them. Garrison's got it all doped out; he figures to outwait us and then vamoose with the dough."

"Meantime if anyone asks him," Cody added, "he's just waitin' for his foreman to show up; good old Bob Baxter."

Two mornings later, Baxter still hadn't shown up, and Garrison came out of his house dressed for town. "I'm saddling up for Steamboat," he told Brady. "Want to come along?"

"Don't mind if I do," Brady said, and began saddling up himself.

Both men kept a straight face. *He knows I'd follow him,* Brady reasoned, *so he beats me to the punch by inviting me to come along.*

All day the two rode south through the forest, stirrup to stirrup, Garrison garbed as a cowman but unarmed, Wayne Brady armed with a deputy's badge and a forty-five gun. Deer crossed the trail ahead of them, and grouse ran peeping through the grass. Garrison had little to say and Brady even less. Bart Conroy's cabin was empty when they passed it. Late in the afternoon they rode into Reinhart's barn in Steamboat Springs.

After the horses were stalled, Brady followed Garrison to the post office and saw the man ask for mail. There wasn't any. Then each man took a room at the Sheridan.

Here in town there was no particular reason to watch Garrison, and Brady had a chance to relax. After supper Jack Camp stopped by the hotel to check with him. "The livery people told me you came in. Anything happen up there?"

"Nothing you could put a finger on," Brady reported. "He's playing cowman, just for a front. Today he rode to town for his mail and I tagged along. Claims he's expecting a cowboy friend named Baxter to ramrod the ranch for him. An old Ora Haley hand, he says. Ever hear of him?"

Camp hadn't. He promised to write Ora Haley at Laramie and ask if a Bob Baxter had ever ridden for him. "I'm like you, Brady; I figure it's just a dummy name. Nothing you can do but tag along when the guy goes back to the park. Odds are he'll lay over here a day or two. Gives you a chance," the undersheriff added with a grin, "to see that gal of yours."

I wish she was. Brady's wistful thought was unspoken. Aloud he asked, "Is Jim Gentry still bird-dogging across the river?"

Camp nodded. "He thinks he's got two leads—both of 'em kinda thin. One's a saloon woman named Franny who hangs around Jeff Silverton's bar. Other's a hard case named Utah Wyckes who usta run with the Tracy–Lant gang in Brown's Park. Wyckes has been arrested twice for horse-thievin', but he alibied his way out of it both times. Totes a gun and is plenty handy with it."

"What about the woman Franny?"

"She came here with Mattie and the two of them worked at Bonnie's house until Mattie went to Denver. You remember Mattie?"

"Yeh, I was on the stage with her when she started to come back here. At Yampa she changed her mind and doubled back east."

"That's right. And Jim Gentry picked up a hint that Franny knows why Mattie changed her mind. So he's been chumming up with Franny, buyin' her a drink now and then. Maybe she'll spill what she knows about Mattie."

"Is that all?"

"That's all. See you tomorrow, Brady."

The hotel barbershop was still open, and when Brady took a walk up the hill his boots were polished and his face freshly shaven. Verna answered his knock at the Bainbridge cottage. Her eyes had a glad welcome as she reached out both hands. "We heard you're in town, Wayne. Uncle Nate's here. He was hoping you'd stop by."

"What about you, Verna? Were *you* hoping I'd stop by?"

"Don't be silly. Of course I was. I'm dying to know what happened up there."

He spent the next half hour in the parlor telling both Verna and her uncle about the stalemate at Slater Park. "We haven't gotten anywhere yet. He's waiting for us to stop watching him. When we do, he figures to pick up the money and be gone."

"But where," Verna wondered, "would he go?"

"To catch a U.P. train at Rawlins would be my guess. There's a trail down Slater Creek to Slater post office and another trail down the Little Snake to Baggs. Indian Tom could guide him that far. At Baggs he could dismiss Tom and ride a stagecoach to Rawlins."

"He'll want a day's rest before riding back to the ranch," Bainbridge reckoned. "You'll go back with him?"

Brady made a grimace. "No way out of it. Takes two to watch him. Cody stays awake while I sleep."

After mulling it over the lawyer made a suggestion. "Why don't you give him a little rope? Let him think he's riding back by himself. Actually you follow along a mile behind him. If he thinks he's alone, he might go straight to his cache, pick up the money, and keep on going. Worth a try, anyway."

Brady agreed that it was. "Nothing to lose by it. So I'll not start till he's been gone half an hour. When he gets into the timber I can narrow the gap. What's been going on here in town, Mr. Bainbridge? You got any fresh ideas?"

"Only one," the lawyer said. "It's about that name Joe you think you heard Bundchu moan out with his last breath. At first we thought he might be putting a name to the killer. But maybe not. We've checked every Joe in the county and none of them fits the case."

"So where does that get us?"

"It's got me stumped," Bainbridge admitted, "except for one possibility. Suppose Otto was tipping us not to the killer but to a witness! Suppose what he tried to gasp out was: 'See Joe'; or 'Ask Joe'; or 'Joe knows.' Something like that—and you caught only the long O sound. How does that strike you?"

"Like smart figuring," Wayne said after a moment's thought. "Have you told Sheriff Farnham?"

Bainbridge nodded. "Now he's rechecking the local Joes, not for a killer, but for someone who knew Bundchu. Must have been plenty of those old-time Hahn's Peakers named Joe. And speaking of Hahn's Peak, there's talk around town about a new gold strike up there. Half a dozen claims filed on it already. Some think it could be the old Karl Janvers gulch that no one could ever find."

Verna asked curiously, "Why would they think that, Uncle Nate?"

"Only because it happened right after Otto Bundchu showed up here, Otto being the only one who knew where it was. This new strike seems to be in an area where nothing was ever found before. Couple of Way's Gulch old-timers, the Pomeroy brothers, have filed there, along with Ambrose Kincaid of Steamboat Springs. Two or three Hahn's Peak men followed them in there. Kincaid's a mining expert who knows as much about that district as anyone else. Hardly a season goes by without someone reporting a new strike up that way. Generally it turns out to be a false alarm." The lawyer shrugged. "If this hadn't happened right after Bundchu got back here, I wouldn't give it a thought."

Bainbridge left them, and Wayne had an intimate hour with Verna. She was warm and confiding; when it was time to go, she let him kiss her goodnight.

He was walking on air as he went back to the hotel. He knew what he wanted now—to somehow get ahead in the world and make a home for Verna. All he had was a hope and a saddle job. But many another man, out here in the stock country, had started with less.

His heart was singing when he stopped at the

Sheridan desk for his key. Instead of a key the clerk handed him a note. "It came by messenger, Mr. Brady, only about ten minutes ago."

The message said:

Wayne:

Join me at Jeff Silverton's bar across the river, soon as you can. Think I've turned up something.

Jim.

XIV

Going to the Reinhart stable for his horse would mean a delay, so Brady took the two-horse hack which at night habitually stood in front of the Sheridan. "The Silverton bar in Brooklyn," he told the driver.

Hauling Steamboat Springs males over to Saloon Row, in the dark of night, was a routine experience for the hackman. He whipped his team five blocks down Lincoln Street to Fifth and then turned downhill to the Yampa River bridge. Hooves clopped on the bridge planks with the current rushing swiftly underneath; then the hack turned left on what was known as the River Road. Lamplights of three saloons and one bagnio gleamed along the southerly side of it. "Did you say Silverton's?" the hackman asked.

"That's right. And you'd better wait for me. I don't expect to be long."

The hack rattled by Big John's, then past Bart Tarkio's. Each hitchrail had saddle horses. Tarkio's place gave off sounds of singing voices, stomping feet and an out-of-tune piano.

"Here you are." The hackman drew up at the last of three saloons.

This one was quieter. But when Brady went inside he found more than a dozen customers. A few were cattle hands. Others looked like mining men, and several could be townsmen from Steamboat Springs who'd slipped over for a little midnight fun.

Two of Bonnie's girls were in sight. One sat on a bar stool drinking with a man Brady recognized as a prominent cattleman from Craig. The other woman was a bit overage for an entertainer— perhaps in her middle forties. Also she was over-dressed and overpainted. She sat with Jim Gentry at a table in the rear corner of the room. No doubt she was the "Franny" mentioned by Camp.

In that case she was the woman who knew why Mattie had changed her mind about returning to Steamboat Springs! Had Jim been able to wheedle anything out of her?

Brady went back and joined them. "Howdy, Jim. Who's your friend? Can I buy you a drink?"

Too late he saw his mistake. The woman was staring at a badge on his vest. Abruptly she stood up and spoke querulously to Jim. "You didn't tell me he's a sheriff!" She started to say something else, then bit her lip and flounced away from them. Almost before they knew it she'd disappeared out of the saloon's back door. From there a few steps uphill would take her to Bonnie's.

Jim made a self-accusing grimace. "Looks like I bobbled it, Wayne. In my note I should have told you to take off that badge. Deputies aren't too popular this side of the river."

"I should have thought of it myself," Brady admitted.

"Lots of hangers-on over here along the Row have got guilty consciences. If they see Franny cozyin' up to a sheriff, they might think she's tellin' tales. That way she'd lose trade. Her kind depend on those guys for a living."

"So we scared her off."

Jim nodded morosely. "I had her thinking I was just a run-of-the-mill cowhand out for a little fun. So after a few drinks she got confidential. She said something about Mattie and I wanted you to hear it too; so that if she denied it later there'd be two of us to pass the story on."

"Pass what story on?"

Jim went to the bar and bought two beers. He handed one of them to Brady. "Mattie and Franny," he reported in an undertone, "worked together at Bonnie's until Mattie went to Denver. They were older than the other girls, and maybe

164

that made them chum up with each other. Each learned a few highlights of the other's past. It seems Mattie started out twenty-two years ago as a waitress in a Tucson, Arizona, restaurant. She wound up as a saloon girl and since then has worked in a dozen cattle and gold towns all over the west."

"Mark Lassiter came from Arizona," Brady remembered. "Did Mattie know him there?"

"Not personally. But he was foreman of a prominent ranch, and so she knew him by sight and reputation. That was when she was waiting tables at a Tucson restaurant. Another man used to come in there every morning for breakfast—a professional gambler, she thought—and she always waited on him. Suddenly he stopped coming. She asked the cook why Mr. So-and-So never came in any more."

"Is that what she called him? Mr. So-and-So?"

"She says the name doesn't matter because it wasn't his real one. The cook told Mattie that the man had to skeedaddle out of the territory because he'd killed a man who knew too much about him. A cold-blood killing, the cook said. He said the killer had slipped up to the man's cabin and shot through an open window—plugged the guy right in the middle of the back."

"Which is what happened to Lassiter," Brady added grimly, "twenty years later."

"Right. And after twenty years Mattie had

almost forgotten about it. Tucson, Gallup, Albuquerque, Soccoro, Trinidad, Leadville, Aspen, Steamboat Springs. Then according to Franny, Mattie came back to their room one night looking scared, or at least, worried. Said she'd just seen a man playing cards in one of the saloons and he'd vaguely reminded her of the gambler who used to eat breakfast in her Tucson restaurant twenty years ago. The Arizona killer! The man would change a lot in that time, so she couldn't be sure.

"Next day she saw him again. But this time it was while she was across the river on a shopping errand. The man was standing on a sidewalk talking and laughing with a group of highly respectable businessmen; they evidently knew him and liked him. So she decided he couldn't possibly be the Arizona killer of 1880. She brushed him out of her mind and a month later went to try her luck in Denver."

Brady thought it over. By the time he'd finished his beer he was able to piece out a reasonable sequence. "Mattie didn't do so well in Denver, at her age, and headed back this way. At Yampa she hears about the Lassiter murder. Lassiter, an ex-Arizonan! The same sneak shot through a window! So maybe she hadn't been mistaken after all. Maybe it *was* the same killer. So why take chances? If he'd do it to Lassiter to keep from being identified, he could treat Mattie the same way. So she changed coaches and headed back east."

"That," Jim agreed, "is about the way Franny figures it. She's got no idea where Mattie is now. Might've gone back to any of her old stands—or to a new one."

"The hack's waiting, Jim. I'll report this to Camp tomorrow and let him take it from there."

"Before you go," Jim suggested, "take a look at that bucko at the head of the bar; the one throwing dice with Jeff Silverton."

Brady turned and saw the man. He had a peaked black hat, a handlebar mustache, and high swarthy cheekbones. Spurred boots and a holstered gun gave him the look of a rangeman; but Brady had never seen him at any of the Routt County roundups.

"He's Utah Wyckes," Jim whispered. "An unconvicted Brown's Park horse thief. We thought maybe he might be the man we're looking for until I ran a check on him. The night you were shot at on the Bainbridge porch Wyckes was in a dice game at Tarkio's from ten till midnight. So we're crossin' him off the list."

"How long has he been hanging around Brooklyn?"

"Two–three weeks. Franny says he wants to buy a saloon. Made an offer to Jeff Silverton, but Jeff turned him down. Jeff's willing to sell but Wyckes can't meet his price."

Brady got to his feet. "If you find out anything else, look me up at the Sheridan tomorrow. Early day-after-tomorrow Garrison's likely to head back to the Slater Park ranch, and if he does I'll have to tag along myself. Thanks for the tip, Jim."

He went out to the waiting hack and was driven across the river to Steamboat. By midnight he was asleep in his room at the hotel.

In the morning he'd just finished breakfast when Garrison came down the stairs. "When," he asked the man, "are you riding back to the park?"

"Early tomorrow. And you?"

"I don't figure to get away that soon," Brady said. "Camp's got a few chores for me here in town. Tell Cody he'll have to carry on by himself till I get there."

"We'll miss you," Garrison said derisively, then went on in to breakfast.

Brady spent an hour at the jail with Camp, relaying information gathered last night from Jim. "We'll pick Franny up and question her," Camp decided. "It's likely she'll deny she ever said anything to Jim."

Brady went next to the Reinhart stable. He gave a hostler there a silver dollar. "Keep my horse grained and ready, Ed. Dale Garrison'll be calling for his mount any time now—maybe early tomorrow. When he does, take a walk over to the Sheridan and tip me off."

"I getcha, Mr. Brady. We heard about you

taggin' that guy. Gonna leave him ride out ahead of you?"

"You've got the idea. But keep mum about it. I want to saddle up about twenty minutes after he does."

At the hotel Brady relaxed. He saw nothing of Garrison for the rest of the morning, but it didn't matter. If he called for his horse, Ed the hostler would hurry over here to tell about it. And here in town the man could do no harm.

Nathan Bainbridge and Verna came by and took him home to lunch with them. He told them about Mattie and Franny and Wyckes, and about the trap he was setting for Garrison.

"Don't let him fool you," the lawyer warned. "He's tricky. For all we know he could be saddling up right now. He could ride as far as Conroy's and stay all night, then go on tomorrow and be four hours ahead of you."

It was a possibility. This very minute there might be a message from the liveryman at the hotel. "Not likely, but I can't chance it," Brady said. "Thanks, Mr. Bainbridge. Goodbye, Verna. See you next time I'm in town."

When he got back to the hotel, there was no message. But to play safe he checked at Reinhart's and made sure Garrison's mount was in a stall there.

Still, a vague worry made him start looking for Garrison. He checked at the man's hotel room, but the room was empty. He looked up and down the street, in stores, barbershops, billiard halls. He even took a walk across the bridge to Saloon Row, but Garrison wasn't in any of the bars.

He began to suspect that Garrison had bought a horse at another stable and had taken off on it.

But late in the afternoon he passed by Milner's bank and saw Garrison at a teller's window. It was just before closing time, and two customers were being served. One, at the withdrawal window, was Garrison. The other, making a deposit at the receiving window, was Jeff Silverton of Brooklyn.

Standing on the sidewalk and looking in, Brady saw a sizable sheaf of currency passed to Garrison. The man tucked it into his billfold and came out to the street. To avoid being seen by him, Brady stepped into the doorway of a gun-shop. A minute later Silverton came out. The saloonman went east, toward the river bridge; Garrison went west, toward the Sheridan Hotel.

After a moment's thought Wayne Brady entered the bank and found Mr. Milner at his desk back of a railing. He sat down by the banker and said bluntly: "Mr. Milner, once we got a court order to make you tell the source of Dale Garrison's deposits. I don't have a court order now—but I could get one. You can save us both time and trouble if you'll tell me whether or not Garrison has just closed out his account."

The banker pulled at his lip for a moment,

then went back and spoke to one of his tellers.

"The answer is affirmative," he said when he rejoined Brady. "Since Mr. Garrison is no longer a client of this bank, I see no reason for not telling you."

"Thanks." Brady hurried away to the jail and relayed the fact to Jack Camp.

The undersheriff cocked an eye. "Got any idea how much he took out?"

"The whole balance, whatever it was. Looked like quite a bundle. Nothing we can do about it, I suppose. It's his money. No law against drawing it out of the bank."

"That's right, Brady. But now we've got more reason than ever to keep an eye on him. And now we know why he really came to town. Not to ask for mail, but to peel his money out of the bank. When he digs up the Slater Park money and takes off, he wouldn't want to leave his bank money behind."

"I couldn't put it better myself, Jack. And don't worry about him giving me the slip. I'll stay close behind him, but out of sight, all the way to the park."

In the morning the call came earlier than Brady expected. It was barely daylight when someone knocked at his door. "He's saddlin' up, Mr. Brady. Better shake a leg."

It was the voice of Ed, the livery stable hostler.

171

By the time Brady was dressed, had swallowed a cup of coffee, and rushed to Reinhart's stable, Dale Garrison had already been gone fifty minutes.

But Brady's mount was saddled, with a carbine in the saddle scabbard, ready for the trail. "He took the Hahn's Peak road, Mr. Brady," a stable boy said.

Brady swung aboard his horse and headed that way himself. It wasn't the only way to Slater Park, but it was the fastest. You could use the Hahn's Peak stage road as far as Big Creek, then veer west from it and cross Elk River, heading on northwesterly to strike the Slater Park trail near Pilot Knob.

An hour out of town, Brady met a lumber wagon from the Sand Mountain sawmill moving south with a load of planks. He hailed the driver. "Did you pass a man on a roan horse? Wears corduroys and a wide-brim hat. He oughta be two–three miles ahead of me."

"Yep, passed him as he was fordin' Big Crik. Spoke to him, but he didn't answer. The roan was blowed a little, like he'd been pushin' it too fast." The driver fixed a gaze on Brady's badge. "Whatsamatter? Is he wanted fer somethin'?"

"Not yet, thanks." Brady spurred on.

Presently he crossed Big Creek himself. A little beyond it he left the stage road and took a branch trail leading westerly toward Long Gulch. It took him to the wide swift riffles of Elk River, which he forded nearly stirrup deep. Beyond that there was only one way to go—up Deep Creek.

Deep Creek had cottonwood timber on both sides, and here there'd been a light rain during the latter part of the night. It had dampened the trail and Brady was able to make out fresh tracks. They were shod hoof marks made since the rain. Because they were heading in his own direction, he was sure they were Garrison's.

After a while he looked closer and saw a double set of prints. Two horsemen had passed here during the last hour or so. They weren't riding side by side, but more or less in tandem. Was Garrison leading a remount? No, because he'd left the Reinhart stable without one; nor had the lumber wagon driver mentioned him as leading a second horse.

Yet definitely someone else besides Garrison had ridden this way early this morning. Was he ahead of Garrison, or following him?

To close the gap, Brady spurred to a faster pace. It was a steady upgrade. Cottonwoods along Deep Creek gave way to cedar and scrub pine. In the distance ahead he could see Pilot Knob, where this route of travel would meet the one heading north toward California and Slater Park.

A mile or so farther on, Brady heard a rifle shot. It came from timber ahead, and was followed by an outcry. Then another shot. After that a gruff voice giving orders. The snort of a horse; then silence.

By that time Brady had forced his horse to a hard run and was snatching his carbine from its scabbard. Half-a-minute later he raced into a clearing where he could see two horses and two men.

One of the men, Dale Garrison, lay face-down on the ground. The other man wore a peaked hat. His high, swarthy cheekbones and handlebar mustache had a familiar look. Almost at once Brady remembered Utah Wyckes, dicing night before last with Jeff Silverton in Brooklyn. Right now he stood by his horse with a rifle in one hand and a fat billfold in the other. He was stripping money from the billfold when Brady burst into sight through the cedars.

The man whipped his rifle up and was shooting by the time Brady hit the sod. He hit it standing and dived forward prone with his carbine level. Two shots whirred over him before he got his first one off.

Utah Wyckes got two more off, both wild. A bullet in the stomach had spoiled his aim. He dropped forward to hands and knees, tried to get up, then collapsed face-down. Brady didn't need to shoot again. Garrison, holding a bleeding head, was getting unsteadily to his feet. He stood in shock, staring as Wayne Brady, leading his horse, came walking toward him.

XV

A noon-high sun found them trailing slowly back toward Steamboat Springs. Brady was leading Wyckes' horse with the man's body draped, uncovered, over the saddle. Garrison, his scalp still throbbing, rode at his stirrup.

Nothing could have been done for Wyckes. The man hadn't lived more than a few minutes. According to Garrison, Wyckes had fired two shots past his ears to frighten him and make him dismount. A whack on the head with a rifle barrel had flattened him, after which Wyckes had helped himself to a billfold.

"How," Garrison wondered presently, "did he know I'd pass by there?"

"Only two ways you can go to Slater Park," Brady reminded him, "and they come together at Pilot Knob. He took his stand there. Either way you went, he knew you had to pass by."

"But how did he know I had . . . ?"

"How did he know you had a wad of money? We can't prove it; but it's a fair guess that he was tipped off by Jeff Silverton. Silverton was making his daily deposit at one window while you were drawing out your money at the other. Wyckes has been dickering to buy Silverton's saloon. He couldn't raise enough cash, so maybe Silverton tipped him where to get some more."

After counting the money and finding that it came to a little less than three thousand dollars, Brady had returned it to Garrison. There was no lawful reason for holding it from him.

"I'm taking you to town," Brady said, "for two reasons. There'll be a coroner's inquest over Wyckes, and we'll both have to testify. And you'd better have Doctor Solandt take a look at your noggin. After that you can go to Slater Park any time you like."

Garrison brightened a little, or pretended to. "Good! While I'm in town maybe Bob Baxter'll show up. Then he can ride up to the ranch with me."

Brady gave him a sidewise look and shook his head resignedly. Such brazenness! Even now, with a cracked head and a dead man riding behind them, he was still sticking to the Baxter story. But like all the rest of his stories, you couldn't prove it wasn't true.

They came finally to the Hahn's Peak stage road and turned south along it. At the Big Creek crossing they met a buckboard with three men in it. The sight of a dead man draped across a saddle made the buckboard people stop.

"A hold-up," Brady explained. "I happened along about that time and we had a shootout. If you see Sheriff Farnham up at the Peak, Mr.

Kincaid, you might tell him about it. He may want to come down for the inquest."

Ambrose Kincaid, holding the reins of the buckboard team, stared at the dead man for a moment before asking, "Who is he?"

"They call him Utah Wyckes. Used to run with the Tracy–Lant gang in Brown's Park." Brady jerked at the lead rope and rode on, Garrison keeping stirrup to stirrup with him. Looking back, he saw the buckboard roll on toward Hahn's Peak.

"A mining engineer?" Garrison asked. "That fellow Kincaid?"

"Something like that," Brady answered. "More like a broker. Sells mining properties on commission. Hires out by the day as a consultant, lots of times. Those two with him look like they might be big city investors or speculators. Kincaid could be trying to put a deal through for them."

A mile further on, they met the afternoon stagecoach heading for Hahn's Peak. Passengers looked out with shocked eyes at what lay jackknifed across the saddle of a led horse. Twice again Brady met travellers and hurried by them to avoid questions. By the time he sighted Steamboat Springs, it was deep twilight, and he'd quite dismissed Ambrose Kincaid from his mind.

In that same deep twilight Kincaid stopped his buckboard in front of Mrs. Larson's hotel in Hahn's Peak. District court having adjourned, he was able to get rooms—one for himself and one for his clients. "Get all the rest you can," he advised them. "Tomorrow night you'll be camping out."

"Where," Benjamin Rumford asked, "is this red-hot property you're going to show us?"

"Wait and see." Kincaid gave them a mysterious smile. "If you don't say it's a humdinger I'll turn in my broker's license."

The other investor, Prentiss, asked impatiently, "Just tell us whether it's a lode or a placer."

"Call it what you want, it's a gold mine," Kincaid assured them. His advantage over Rumford was that twice before the man had consulted him profitably. As for Horace Prentiss, he'd made a fortune at Cripple Creek and lost it at Creede; now he was straining at the bit to recoup his losses elsewhere.

The pair were Denver men, old clients, and Kincaid had written them that if they'd come to Steamboat Springs, he'd show them a "good thing": something they could triple their money on in a season. And since he'd served them well before, both men had come promptly by train and stage to Routt County.

"The way you talk," Rumford remarked during supper, "a fella 'd think you'd stumbled on the old Karl Janvers placer." The story of Karl Janvers had long been a legend among Colorado mining men.

"Maybe I have," Kincaid said cryptically. "Take a look at it and judge for yourselves."

"When do we start?"

"Sunup. It's only a two–three hour drive from here. And what you'll see there, gentlemen, is raw gold and plenty of it."

At sunup they were on their way. These city men were too soft for saddle travel, and so again they rode in a buckboard. In it were two bedrolls, a small tent, and provisions for two days and two nights. Kincaid's saddle mule, with a lead rope tied to the endgate, came trotting along behind.

Ben Rumford looked surprised when he saw they were heading west. "Nothing but sheep country over this way, I always thought." Having been to the Hahn's Peak district several times before, he knew that all earlier strikes had been made north and east of the main camp.

Kincaid chuckled. "That's what everybody thought, up till now. Wait till you see the *Flamingo*."

After leaving the Columbine road, they had to pick their way over a route meant only for saddle travel. However, fresh wheel tracks proved that other vehicles had passed this way lately. One of them would be the wagonload of lumber hauled to Oliver Creek by the cabin contractor Kincaid had employed. By now the cabin should be well under way.

179

"What's the latest word," he asked his clients, "about the Moffatt line?"

"She's acomin'," Prentiss assured him. "They've just let a contract for the grading of thirty-six miles from Boulder Park to Kremmling. Three hundred men are at work there already."

"I've got it from top sources," Rumford added, "that they plan a tunnel through the divide and figure on running trains into Steamboat Springs by this time next year. Rails at Steamboat'll mean a short ore haul from Hahn's Peak. Mines that can't break even now'll be showing a profit, once the track gets into Routt County."

They didn't need to tell Ambrose Kincaid that. It was the very reason why he'd hung onto his stock in three mines which long ore hauls had almost shut down—the *Tom Thum*, the *Elkhorn*, and the *Minnie D.*

He knew too that these clients of his wanted to get in on the ground floor early, before the coming of the Moffatt line made mineral properties at Hahn's Peak shoot upward in value.

"Have you set a price on this *Flamingo* claim of yours?" Prentiss asked him.

"No. I'm going to let *you* set the price. Ever hear of the Pomeroy brothers, Hank and Frank?"

Prentiss hadn't, but Rumford had. "Met 'em at Way's Gulch last time I was up here. A pair of Bible-reading teetotalers, as I remember."

"That's right. They came here in Sixty-eight

with Hahn and Way and Doyle. Right now I've got them working the *Flamingo* for me on shares. All I ask you men is for you to camp there a couple of days and watch them."

"Watch 'em work?"

"Watch 'em pan gold. Ask 'em a few questions. Weigh the dust they've taken out in the last week. Then go to Hahn's Peak and ask if anyone ever knew them to lie or cheat. Then come down to Steamboat and make me an offer."

More than that Kincaid wouldn't tell them. He bumped the buckboard on another mile, then topped a wooded ridge and dropped down into the head of Oliver Creek.

It was no longer a deserted wilderness. People were there—not only the Pomeroy brothers and a crew of cabin builders, but a dozen miners who'd stampeded over from Hahn's Peak to file adjacent claims.

"We couldn't help it," Frank Pomeroy said to Kincaid as he drove up. "We never let out anything. But those fellows saw us at work and they talked." He thumbed toward the cabin contractor and his helper.

"And did their eyes pop out!" Hank Pomeroy added with a grin, "when they saw what we were panning. Word of it got to the Peak—and here they came!"

"No jumpers?" Kincaid inquired anxiously.

"No jumpers," Hank said matter-of-factly. The

Pomeroys not only had a Bible. They had a pair of shotguns and thirty years' experience in standing off claim jumpers. "All they did was stake claims of their own above and below ours. Haven't heard of 'em hittin' any pay sand yet."

The walls of the log cabin were already halfway up. Lumber for rafters and flooring was piled nearby. On the creekbank the Pomeroys had pitched their tent. Close by it, Kincaid put up another tent for his clients.

"They'll be boarding with you a couple of days," he told Hank. "I may sell out to them if they make me a fair offer. Please show them every courtesy."

"What about you, Mr. Kincaid. Will you be staying here too?"

"No. I'll head back to the Peak by saddle and leave the buckboard here for Mr. Rumford and Mr. Prentiss. When they're ready they can drive it back to town and then ride a stagecoach to Steamboat."

"In that case," Hank suggested, "we'd better divvy what we've panned to date. Come on in and we'll weigh it out."

He led the way into their living tent, and Kincaid beckoned to his clients. "Come along, you fellows. I want you to see this too."

Rumford and Prentiss exchanged cautious looks. Both were alert for a trick. The oldest trick of all was the salting of a gold mine in order to swindle an investor. But they followed Kincaid into the tent.

It was a nine by twelve shelter with two bedroll pallets, a small table, and an oaken chest. The chest had a padlock which Frank Pomeroy unlocked. From it he took a dust scales and a buckskin pouch. The pouch had gold dust and small nuggets. These he poured onto the scales.

"Read it yourself, Mr. Kincaid."

The scales pointer indicated 58 and one half ounces.

"Seven days panning for two men!" Hank announced jubilantly. "And we haven't even put up a sluice trough yet."

"Half of it's yours, Mr. Kincaid." Frank scooped gold back into the pouch until what was left on the scales weighed exactly 29 and one quarter ounces. He hand the pouch to Ambrose Kincaid.

Rumford exclaimed: "I just can't believe it, Kincaid! Fifty-eight troy ounces comes to a little more than a thousand dollars—about seventy-five dollars per man-day. Nothing like that's happened since Virginia City."

"What about Karl Janvers?" Hank Pomeroy countered.

"Are you telling us," Rumford challenged, "that this is the Janvers gulch?"

"It could be," Hank insisted. "It's either the Janvers gulch or one just like it. Frank, go put on a pot of coffee."

Rumford and Prentiss moved apart, whispering, half fearful of being tricked, half fearful of missing out on a bonanza. While coffee was boiling, Kincaid went for a talk with his cabin contractor. "Finish up as quick as you can," he told the man, and gave him a check for half the contract price.

The buckboard team was off-harnessed and picketed in hillside grass. "The Pomeroys'll hook up for you," he told Rumford, "when you're ready to leave. Meantime they'll board you. I know what you're thinking right now—that maybe we've salted some creek gravel to fool you. But stick around a few days with your eyes open. Pick out your own stretch of sand and tell them to dip there. Dip a few pans yourself if you like."

The prospective investors were still dubious when Kincaid left them. But he knew they were too curious, as well as too covetous, to quit the place until they were sure one way or the other. A few days of seeing with their own eyes should convince them.

After a final word with the Pomeroys, Kincaid stepped into the saddle of his mule and rode easterly through the woods toward Hahn's Peak.

He was reasonably sure that the Denver men would make him an offer. Whatever the offer was, he'd double their figure and perhaps in the end split the difference.

Cash in the bank, for Ambrose Kincaid, was

always better than gold in a gulch. Twice in his life he'd had to make a fast getaway from one part of the country to another. Once from Maryland to Arizona; once from Arizona to Colorado. Any day or hour, he might have to do it again. Which meant that he'd better keep his assets fluid.

He was thinking of this when he rode into Hahn's Peak and found the daily stage from Steamboat Springs pulling up there. Among the passengers getting off were reporters from both the Steamboat Springs weeklies.

They hailed Kincaid as he rode by on his mule.

The *Pilot* man got to him first. "Just a minute, Mr. Kincaid. What about this new gold strike out west of here? Over by the Nipple."

"Is it true," the *Sentinel* man followed up, "that it could be the old lost placer that Karl Janvers used to clean up on?"

Kincaid gave them a cryptic smile and a shrug. "About whether it's the Janvers gulch or not, your guess is as good as mine. Gold is wherever you find it."

"You made the discovery strike yourself, they say. Is that right?"

Kincaid curled a tongue in his cheek. Now that his title was solidly filed and he had buyers on the string, the more publicity he got, the better. "I was lucky, boys. Happened by there and lay belly-down for a drink. Saw color in the sand and scratched out a nugget. So I staked a claim and turned it over to the Pomeroy brothers to work on shares. They've done pretty well so far. Just rode over there to collect my first week's split."

"Mind showing it to us, Mr. Kincaid?"

"I don't see why not. Take a look." Kincaid brought a small buckskin pouch from his pocket and let them heft the weight of it. The *Sentinel* man opened it for a pinch. It was the real thing all right.

"Golly-Gee-Whoppers! You mean this is just your half of a week's work by two men?"

"That's it. Why don't you go over there and see for yourself?" Kincaid spurred his mule on to the stage barn. A smile creased his face as he unsaddled. It meant that both weeklies would have big headlines in their next issues. Headlines which would later be reprinted in Denver, Colorado Springs, Leadville, and Georgetown. All of it grist to his own mill.

It would pull other speculators and investors in to bid against Prentiss and Rumford. More than that, it would tend to boom the entire Hahn's Peak mineral district. Faith would be restored in what was beginning to be thought of as a ghost camp. Stocks in other mines, unsaleable now, would suddenly find bidders. Ambrose Kincaid had small blocks of stock in three which he wanted to cash in on—the *Tom Thum*, the *Elkhorn*, and the *Minnie D.*

XVI

During supper at Mrs. Larson's hotel he listened to talk from passengers who'd just come from Steamboat on the stage. Most of it was about a coroner's inquest held this morning—dealing with a gunfight near Pilot Knob in which a would-be robber named Wyckes had lost his life.

The verdict had been prompt: "Death by gunfire while in the act of committing a felony and while resisting arrest by a deputy county sheriff."

The *Pilot* and the *Sentinel* men were at the table, and both had covered the inquest. "Only mystery about it," the *Pilot* man offered, "is why Dale Garrison would draw three thousand dollars out of the bank and head up toward Slater Park with it. His story is that he bought the Lassiter ranch, and so now he needs to stock it. Says an experienced ranch foreman named Baxter is about to join him. They'll ride around to other ranches, he says, and pick up bargains wherever they find 'em. A few horses here, a few cows there. Says the owners won't know him, so he'll need cash."

The *Sentinel* men scoffed at it. "Everybody who believes that, stand on his head. It's too late in the season to stock a ranch at that altitude. And no one ever heard of this Baxter man. I talked with Jack Camp, and he thinks Garrison's getting set for a run-out. The talk is he's got seven thousand dollars of Mark Lassiter's money cached up there. Only reason he hasn't made a run with it is that the sheriff's got a couple of watchdogs up there keepin' eyes on him."

Kincaid listened without comment. Was there an angle in it, somewhere, for himself? A ten-thousand-dollar cash stake at a wilderness ranch was something to think about. Three thousand in Garrison's wallet and seven thousand more buried nearby! He'd had no dealings with Garrison, but he'd often seen the man around town. He lived at the Sheridan—but without known means of support. Definitely a city type, a comfort lover, just the opposite of a rugged frontier type who'd want to start ranching in the wilds of Routt County.

A masquerader himself, Ambrose Kincaid was peculiarly apt at seeing through the masks of others. He'd be willing to bet that Garrison had no faint thought of operating a cattle ranch. He was up there for some other purposes—more than likely the one suggested by Undersheriff Camp: to reclaim and make off with hidden money.

Kincaid went to bed and for a while lay wakeful, his mind reviewing his past and planning his future. He thought back to the University of Maryland, where more than twenty years ago he'd graduated with a degree in mining engineering. A liking for draw poker had been his downfall; in a game at the Lord Baltimore Hotel he'd quarreled with a man over a jackpot and killed him. It had forced him to run, change his name, and hide in a place called Tombstone, Arizona. Although it was a silver town, he'd been afraid to practice as a mining engineer there, for it would have helped to identify him as a fugitive from Maryland. So he'd made a living with the only other skill he had—cards—by taking a job as dealer in Wyatt Earp's Oriental Saloon.

It hadn't lasted long. Soon after that the Earp brothers, having wiped out a rival faction in a shootout at the O.K. Corral, had been forced to leave the territory on the run. For another dealing job Kincaid had moved seventy miles down the range to Tucson, and there an old Marylander had crossed his path—a man who could point a finger and bring Maryland law down on him.

A crisis he'd averted with a sneak shot through a cabin window.

After that another forced flight, this time to the loneliest place he could find, far from railroads: Routt County, Colorado. There the close-by mining community of Hahn's Peak had tempted him to reclaim his original skill—practice as a consulting mining expert and broker. By then enough time had passed so that the hue and cry from Maryland had died down.

But the hue and cry from Arizona hadn't. Three times a potential Arizona witness had crossed his path: Mark Lassiter, the woman Mattie, and Otto Bundchu, or rather Little Joe, who'd been a cellmate of Bundchu's. Also, an old rock-pecker named Yancy had happened along during Kincaid's run after dealing with Lassiter. All had been dealt with except Mattie, and she had, been frightened out of the country.

The next hazard, Kincaid foresaw, would be the coming of the Moffatt line to Steamboat Springs. Or rather it would be both a blessing and a hazard. It would boom Hahn's Peak properties and let him cash in handsomely. On the other hand, it would bring droves of people from the Outside—and among them there could be another witness to the past of a man who now called himself Ambrose Kincaid.

At noon the next day he stepped off the stage-coach in front of the Sheridan Hotel in Steamboat and headed down the walk toward his office. On the way he passed Milner's bank and turned in there.

Mr. Milner was at his desk, and Kincaid handed him a buckskin pouch, small but heavy. "Please weigh this for me," he said, "and credit it to my account."

Deposits of the kind were routine at this bank. Posted on the wall at all times was the current price of gold. Today it was $17.66 per ounce. Every bank in the mining counties of Colorado posted such a notice and accepted such deposits.

Mr. Milner's only surprise was in the source and the amount of this one. His cashier, after weighing it, said it came to 29 and one quarter ounces. "Figures out $516.55, Mr. Kincaid. Got your pass book with you?"

The deposit was entered in the book and Kincaid went on to his office.

From his locked desk he took three stock certificates, and on the back of each he signed his name, effectively endorsing the certificate for transfer. Next he took up a week-old Denver paper and turned to the financial section. One column listed current values of industrial stocks on the New York Stock Exchange. Another gave current grain prices at the Chicago Pit. Still another posted current bids for milling stocks at the Colorado Mine Exchange, located on the top floor of the Mining Exchange Building in Colorado Springs.

Nearly every active incorporated gold, silver, or copper mine in the Rocky Mountains was listed there; so much per share bid, so much per share asked. Some of the properties, now at low ebb, were quoted at only a few cents per share.

The *Elkhorn* in Whisky Park wasn't listed at all; the *Tom Thum* and the *Minnie D* could be had for less than a dollar per share.

It should be different, though, after word had spread of a new placer bonanza in the district.

Always in mining history, a boom in one camp had tended to accelerate optimism as to all other properties in the same area.

So Kincaid wrote an instruction to the Board of Governors of the Mining Exchange, Mining Exchange Building, Colorado Springs, telling them to sell for him, at market, the enclosed three certificates of stock. He sealed them in an envelope, together with the letter of instruction. He stamped the letter but for the time being did not mail it.

Instead, he locked it in a desk drawer. He'd wait till stories about the *Flamingo* came out in the *Pilot* and the *Sentinel*, and then wait until the stories were reprinted on the financial page of the *Rocky Mountain News* at Denver. A day after that he could mail these certificates and look forward to a bullish sale.

He went up the street to the Bon Ton Restaurant for lunch, then stopped at the post office for his mail. Two of the letters were from old clients and required answers. Back in his office, Kincaid was penning the answers when someone knocked at his door.

"Come in."

The man who entered was tall, lean, and black-thatched, with shrewd dark eyes and a bony face. Kincaid had never had dealings with him, but knew him by reputation as one of Routt County's leading lawyers.

"Mr. Bainbridge!" he greeted cautiously. "What can I do for you?"

The caution was because he knew that Bainbridge was attorney for the Lassiter estate; more than that he'd been hosting Wayne Brady on the night a bullet had smashed into a porch post at his cottage. Did this call have anything to do with those facts?

"I won't bother you but a minute," the attorney said. "Just dropped in because they say you're well acquainted with people up around Hahn's Peak. Do you know any of these men?" He laid a list of nine names on Kincaid's desk.

Kincaid knew or had heard of all. Seven were miners, one was a bartender and one was a stable hand. All nine had the same first name, "Joseph."

"I got some of the names from the county tax rolls," Bainbridge explained, "some from Sheriff Farnham, some from Stage Driver Bill Marshman, some from County Clerk Withers: Can you add any to the list? Anybody else up there named Joe?"

"There's a trapper in Whisky Park," Kincaid told him, "named Joe Webber."

"Thanks." Bainbridge added the name to his list.

"What's the idea?" Kincaid was still cautious and more than a little worried.

The frankness with which the attorney answered dispelled some of the worry. Clearly Kincaid himself wasn't under suspicion. "We think that

Otto Bundchu, just before he died, mentioned a name something like Joe. We've checked all the Joes around Steamboat Springs and none of them could have had any connection with Bundchu. So now we're checking on Hahn's Peak people. Hahn's Peak, after all, was Bundchu's original stamping ground."

"I see!" Kincaid said with a degree of relief. "Well, that sounds like a pretty good idea. If I think of any more Joes up that way I'll let you know."

"Thanks again." Bainbridge had been standing all the while. Now he picked up his list and left the office.

Kincaid looked in a wall mirror and saw a bead of sweat on his forehead. He mopped it away and then took stock. A really alarming thing about the situation was that Bainbridge had used the pronoun "we," meaning himself and the law authorities of Routt County. The sheriff, the undersheriff and the district attorney were not, in Kincaid's opinion, either brilliant or imaginative. But Nathan Bainbridge was definitely both.

And Bainbridge, as attorney for the Lassiter estate, had a professional interest in getting at the truth. He'd already checkmated Dale Garrison by posting guards up at the Slater Park ranch. Now he was keen enough, and aggressive enough, to follow up on the dying outcry of Otto Bundchu.

Fortunately the man Brady, rushing into the

room, hadn't caught all of it. Apparently he'd caught only a single syllable that sounded like Joe. The full outcry, Kincaid knew only too well, had been, *"See Little Joe!"*

So now Bainbridge was nose-down to the trail of an unknown Joe. He'd tried Steamboat Springs and Brooklyn; now he was trying Hahn's Peak. Would he finally get wise and try the area of Bundchu's last residence—the State penitentiary at Canon City?

If he did he'd inevitably turn up an ex-cellmate of Bundchu's known as "Little Joe," who'd once tended bar for Wyatt Earp in Tombstone, Arizona, and who'd later run with the Tracy–Lant gang in Brown's Park.

The possibilities were ominous for Kincaid. Always there'd been a chance of sudden exposure, and for that reason, some years ago, he'd opened a checking account in the First National Bank of Rawlins, Wyoming. His balance there was, and always had been, just one hundred dollars. His back-door money, he called it, if worse came to the worst.

From Steamboat Springs there were two doors to the Outside—a front door and a back door. If you left by the front door you rode a stagecoach to Wolcott and there changed to a Denver & Rio Grande train. If you left by the back door you rode a stage to Hahn's Peak and from there rode horseback north to the Little Snake River and down the Little Snake to Baggs; from Baggs you could ride a stagecoach some sixty miles north to Rawlins on the Union Pacific.

If a man were forced to use that back door suddenly, out of banking hours, he might arrive at Rawlins without the price of a train ticket in pocket. Against such a possibility, Kincaid had hedged. The hundred dollars planted at Rawlins would buy the ticket.

But with very little left over, so he'd better sweeten that Rawlins bank account a bit, he decided. Kincaid wrote a check on the Milner bank here for about half of his present balance, making it payable to the First National Bank of Rawlins, Wyoming. He clipped on a note to the Rawlins bank, instructing them to credit it to his account.

Before the afternoon was over he'd mailed the note and the check to Rawlins. Just in case things got too hot here, all of a sudden, and he had to make a fast exit by the back door.

XVII

Walt Cody and Indian Tom were pitching horse-shoes in front of the barn when Wayne Brady and Dale Garrison returned to the Slater Park ranch. This time they rode abreast, and from a distance would have seemed to be comrades rather than lawman and suspect. Cody and Indian Tom might have been bunkmates on the same crew.

After mounts were unsaddled and corraled, Garrison and his cook went to the main house while Brady and Walt went to the bunk cabin.

"The first time he started back up here," Brady explained over coffee, "I followed a piece behind him; giving him some rope to see what he'd do. But no use trying that trick a second time; he'd be leery after what happened before. So I just sided him stirrup to stirrup, all the way. What happened up here while I was gone?"

"Not a thing," Walt reported. "Everything cozy. Fact is, I ate up at the main house with Tom. Him and me got along like buddies. He's kinda dumb, but I figure he's on the level. Whatever Garrison's up to, I'll bet Tom doesn't know anything about it. Cook and guide, that's all."

"Garrison's got a walletful of money, Walt. Drew out his whole account from the bank. That's the real reason he went to town. When he digs

197

up the Lassiter money he'll have quite a stake."

"Which he's a cinch to take off with," Cody agreed, "except for us watchin' him. Wonder how the heck he figgers to get rid of us."

"*Quien sabe*? He's not the kind who'd try to outgun us. I doubt if he even has a gun. But he's got time; more time than we have. One of these days the county'll get tired of paying us to sit around here. Soon as we're gone, he can pick up the money and light out."

"He won't get far on that roan of his," Walt said, "unless he grains it."

Wayne Brady nodded shrewdly. "And we won't get far chasing him unless we grain ours. Tell you what, Walt. You'd better ride to Hahn's Peak tomorrow and buy some oats."

The Withers store at Hahn's Peak was the nearest place where grain could be bought. It was ten forest miles east of here and rough going, but the round trip could be made in a day.

Walt grinned. "I getcha. We grain our horses but not his. If Garrison runs and we chase, his horse 'll play out and ours won't."

Five saddle mounts and one pack mare were on the ranch now. Brady, Cody, Garrison, and Indian Tom had each arrived by saddle, Tom leading a pack animal. Mark Lassiter's saddle horse, at the time of his death, had been in the corral here, all other Lassiter livestock having been sold. Of the six animals, four were usually turned loose in a meadow pasture back of the barn. The other two were usually in the corral and fed hay from the loft.

But for an endurance run a horse would need grain.

"When you go to the Peak tomorrow, Walt, ride your horse and lead Lassiter's. Load two one-hundred-pound sacks of oats on Lassiter's horse and lead it back here. We'll keep the grain in the bunk cabin and feed it only to our own mounts."

Cody chuckled. "And Garrison being a tenderfoot, he won't even know how much difference that 'll make. A grain-fed horse can out-travel a grass-fed horse, or a hay-fed horse, ten to one."

Cody kept watch during the night while Brady slept. And soon after breakfast Cody was off, riding his own horse and leading Lassiter's.

Brady spent a quiet day. He saw nothing of Garrison and had an idea that the man was sleeping off yesterday's ride. Once he saw Indian Tom carry a bucket of water from the well. Brady himself went to the barn twice, morning and evening, to pitch hay down from the loft into a manger. "This time tomorrow," he promised his mount, "you'll be munching oats."

An irrigation lateral ran through a corner of the corral, so that coralled stock could get water at will.

By sundown Cody was back with two bulging

sacks draped across his led horse. "Big excitement at the Peak," he reported.

"About what?"

"New placer strike on Oliver Creek. Streak of pay sand so rich that some people think it's the old Karl Janvers gulch. The Pomeroy brothers are workin' it, and cleaning up."

"I heard talk about it at Steamboat," Brady remembered. "Seems a mining engineer named Kincaid staked it, then leased it to the Pomeroys. Hahn's Peak's waited a long time for a break like that."

"It sure has. Larson's hotel's overflowin' again. Every time we think that town's dead and buried, somethin' happens to wake it up again."

"Hear any other news?"

"Nope—I had to leave before the stage from Steamboat got in."

This time Brady took the night watch and let Cody sleep. In the morning he napped while Walt grained two of the horses and gave them a rubdown. And still the main house showed no sign of Garrison. Except for a wisp of smoke from the kitchen chimney and Tom's occasional appearance on some minor chore, the ranch house would have seemed deserted.

A pair of mallards circled the park and alighted on the trickle of water called Slater Creek. "If I had a shotgun," Walt said, "I'd go bag 'em."

Brady pointed. "Tom's got one, and there he

goes." They saw Tom emerge from the house with a shotgun, stalk the ducks, and fire twice as they rose squawking from the water. He missed one, got the other.

The sight of a firearm prompted Brady to clean his own. The saddles were at the barn, but the saddle carbines were here at the bunk cabin. With a ramrod and rag he cleaned Cody's rifle and his own.

"We've got everything on 'em, Walt. Our grained horses against their grass horses; our rifles and six-guns against one shotgun. Not that we'll need 'em. But I'd sure like to get some action. This cat-and-mouse game is getting on my nerves."

"Who's that comin'?" Walt wondered, pointing south. A horseman had come out of the timber and was riding toward them.

A minute more and they recognized Jim Gentry. Jim, looking fagged from a forced ride, came up and off-saddled. His saddle scabbard had a carbine, and his belt had a forty-five gun.

"Got a cup of coffee? I pushed along pretty hard and I'm bushed."

"Thought we had you planted at Brooklyn," Brady said. "Anything happen over there?"

"They froze me out," Jim explained. "After that misfire you and I had with Franny, you with a badge on, everybody over there figured me for a snoop. They don't like snoops. Jeff Silverton won't even serve me at his bar any more. Big John took my loft cot away and there I was, out in the cold."

Brady nodded. He could understand that Jim had outlived his usefulness over there. "So you're out scouting for a ranch job again," he suggested.

"Nope. Feed me a cup of coffee and I'll give you an earful."

With coffee in hand he explained why he'd made a fast forced ride to Slater Park. "Last night I was in Tarkio's bar. Three buckos I'd never seen before were killing a quart. I asked one of Bonnie's gals who they were, and she said she'd heard they were from Brown's Park. That's ninety miles west, and Brown's Park people don't often get to Steamboat. It's handier for them to do their drinkin' at Craig.

"These three looked like fine upstanding horse thieves if I ever saw any. They were heeled with holster guns, and when they finished the quart and went out to their horses, I tagged along. Their saddles had scabbard guns. I stood just around the corner of the building and listened in on 'em. A good thing I did; because they were talkin' about you, Wayne."

Brady cocked an eye. "Me? I don't know anyone in Brown's Park."

"They didn't mention your name," Jim admitted. "But I heard one of them say, 'We owe him a slug.' Another said: 'Two slugs; one for Wyckes and one for Hix.' Then the other fella said, 'He's up in Slater Park right now.' So I saddled up and made time this way myself."

Brady thought it over a minute, then asked, "Who's Hix?"

"I was curious about that myself," Jim said; "so I looked it up. Hix is a horse thief in jail at Hahn's Peak; the one you pounced on from a loft that time he was making a getaway."

Brady nodded. "I remember. I rode all the way from Wolcott on the stage with him. You tellin' me he's a Brown's Parker?"

"All I know is what those three buckos said at Tarkio's hitchrail last night. Sounds to me like all five of 'em belonged to the same gang; what's left of the old Tracy–Lant gang of Brown's Park outlaws. They owe you a slug, one of 'em says. Two slugs, another says; one for Wyckes and one for Hix." Jim refilled his coffee cup, then added: "Didn't want 'em to catch you by surprise, three rifles against two. So I fetched my own along."

"Makes us even," Walt Cody said grimly. "Three agin three."

Jim Gentry stood in the open door and looked south. "For all we know," he warned, "they could be only a shake or two behind me."

Brady doubted it. "It could 've been that quart of whisky talking for them. Brag talk at a bar. Maybe by now they've forgotten all about it and are on their way back to Brown's Park."

Just the same, he checked the loads in both his carbine and his belt gun. The bunk cabin had three bunks, and Jim tossed his saddle pack on the unused one. Then he led his horse to the barn and put feed out for it, and by the time he was back Brady had organized three eight-hour watches.

"We'll have to stand guard in both directions," he said, "around the clock. We keep an eye on the house, in case Garrison slips out to his money cache; and we keep a sharp lookout for the three Brown's Parkers. I'll take the dog watch, midnight till eight in the morning. Walt, you take the day watch—eight till four. Jim, that leaves you on from four in the afternoon till midnight."

As soon as Walt had cooked up a beans-and-bacon supper, the routine was established. Nightfall found Brady and Cody sleeping while Jim sat on the bunk cabin steps with a carbine across his knees. Lamplight glowed at a window of the main house. Frogs croaked from the creeklet; occasion-ally a horse champed in the barn; otherwise the night was soundless.

At about ten o'clock the house window darkened, indicating that both Garrison and his cook had gone to bed. The bunk cabin too was dark except for the glow of Gentry's cigaret. He kept his post till a few minutes past midnight, then went in to waken Brady.

For the next eight hours it was Brady who sat on

the steps with a rifle. There was bright moonlight with stars studding the sky. Light enough for a night ride; but with each passing hour Brady felt more and more certain that what Jim had heard at Tarkio's hitchrail was merely whisky talk; brag talk. By now those three gunnies could be halfway back to Brown's Park.

A star-bright night and a quiet one. Black lines around the rim of Slater Park were walls of lodgepole pine, where the forest edged the park on all sides. After a long silence Brady heard the hoot of an owl; still later he heard the bugle of a bull elk off to the north, toward Shield Mountain. The next sound he heard, just as dawn was breaking, was the creaking of a pulley rope at the well, Indian Tom was drawing himself a bucket of breakfast water.

When the light brightened, Brady made a fire in the bunk cabin stove and put coffee on. While it was heating he went to the corral with a pail of oats. All but three of the horses were out in pasture. Brady took two of the three to stalls and fed each a ration of grain. They were Jim's mount and his own. The one still in the corral was Garrison's.

Back at the cabin he found Cody up and mixing pancake batter. They let Jim Gentry sleep till eight.

"Anything doing?" Jim asked when he pulled on his boots.

"Not yet." Walt flipped a pancake. "But keep your powder dry. Remember what those guys said about owin' Brady two slugs—one for Hix and one for Wyckes."

Brady turned in and went promptly to sleep. They didn't waken him at noon. Early in the afternoon, the sound of a complaining voice aroused him, and he swung his legs from the bunk, reaching for his rifle.

But it was only an altercation between Dale Garrison and Walt Cody. Brady, in his sock feet, joined in.

"Look here, Brady," Garrison protested. "This is my ranch. I bought it in fee simple. What kind of a deal is this, anyway? It was bad enough having two of you here, trespassing, eating my hay out of my barn. Now there's three of you. When are you going to clear out?"

"We'll clear out," Brady promised him, "soon as we find out who killed Lassiter and what happened to his money. Remember I'm a county deputy, and the law sent me here to look for evidence. Haven't found any yet, but I keep looking. May take all fall and winter. Far as your hay goes, put in a bill to the county and if it's fair, they'll pay it."

Garrison gave him a sullen stare. "What about these other two men?" he demanded.

"One's cooking for me; the other spells me while I sleep. For instance, if I was asleep in the middle of the night and he heard you saddling up at the barn, he'd roust me out and I'd go down there to see where you're going."

"I'm not going anywhere."

"Fine. Long as you don't, we won't bother you. And if that ramrod of yours, Baxter, rides in, we won't bother him either." Brady drooped an eyelid in the direction of Walt Cody.

Garrison flushed, started to say something, then whipped around and walked back to the house.

Walt gave a chuckle. "Mad as a wet hen, that guy. Nothing he can do about it, either." It was nearly four in the afternoon, and he began getting ready for bed.

By the time Walt was asleep, Jim had begun his four-till-midnight watch.

Brady sat on a step near him and said: "No use of our feeding out any more of Garrison's hay than we can help. So we'll just keep up one horse at a time. You can turn yours out to pasture and grain mine."

Jim took a scoop of oats and walked down to the stable. He was out of sight in the stable when Brady saw three riders come out of the forest to the south. They rode toward this cabin at a trot.

He'd never seen them before. Three shabby, shaggy men with the stock of a carbine slanting up from each saddle scabbard.

Over his shoulder Brady called to Cody. "On your feet, Walt. We've got visitors."

He had to repeat the call before Cody heard and

popped out of his bunk. In his sock feet Walt came to the door and peered out. He could see three horsemen less than half-a-mile off and heading this way. "Where's Jim?"

"In the barn, Walt. He didn't take his rifle with him. Only his belt gun."

In less than a minute Cody had his boots on and his own rifle in hand. He pumped a shell into the chamber and stood in the open door directly behind Brady.

The three riders came on at a brisk trot.

"I know the middle one," Walt whispered. "The one with red whiskers. He shot up a Craig saloon one time and had to do ninety days in the Hahn's Peak jail. Name's Harper."

Harper was the shortest and shabbiest of the three. They were sure to be the three Brown's Parkers Jim had seen at Tarkio's bar. Jim had described them as: "Fine upstanding horse thieves if ever I saw any." The tall, thin man on Harper's left had a sallow, sunken beardless face. The one on his right was big, thick-necked, and beefy at the middle. All three had cartridge belts and holster guns. They may have been drunk night before last, but right now they were cold sober.

They reined up in front of the bunk cabin, not dismounting. There they held their horses in a row facing Brady and not more than eight paces from the bunk cabin steps.

The red-whiskered man did the talking.

"Know where we can find a fella named Brady?"

"You're looking at him," Brady said as he stood up. He didn't think they'd make a go for guns. Not just yet, anyway. They'd want to know what the odds were first. Who and how many were up at the main house. Who, if anyone, was in the barn?

The beefy man spoke next. "You mean you're Brady?"

"That's right. I'm Brady. You wanted to see me about something?"

The three exchanged looks and Harper gave a slight nod. It must have been a prearranged signal, for the big, beefy man kneed his mount a few paces to the left, widening the space between himself and the others. At the same time the tall, thin man shifted to the right. It would give them an advantage if it came to a shootout—two men bunched in a doorway against three outside and widely spaced.

The decision seemed to be Harper's. Harper fixed a slitted-eyed stare on Brady for a moment, then looked at the main house, where a wisp of chimney smoke indicated occupants. "Is that tenderfoot still up there? Him and his halfbreed cook?"

"They're there," Brady told him. Evidently these men had heard about the general situation up here; about Garrison buying the ranch and occupying it with a cook—under suspicious observation by Brady and Cody posted in the bunk cabin. That much could be common gossip in town by now.

What they didn't know was that Jim Gentry had arrived to reinforce them and was now in the barn.

They'd have nothing but contempt, Brady guessed, for Garrison and his cook. They'd know Garrison wasn't the kind who'd take part in a bunkhouse gunfight. And even if he did he wouldn't be on the side of Brady.

The long, skinny man, sitting his saddle well to the right of Harper, spoke for the first time. "You've got a long nose, Brady."

Brady kept his eyes fixed on Harper. He had a feeling that the next nod of Harper's head would signal a go for guns.

"You used it twice," the big, thick-necked man put in. "Once when you stuck it into Hix's business; and once when you fouled up Wyckes."

"So we gotta make sure," Harper added with a nod of his head, "that you don't use it again." He made a snap draw and both his siders did the same.

Brady was ready for it. He shot from the hip, not at Harper but at the long, thin man. Walt Cody, flanking him in the doorway, got off two fast shots before dropping to his knees to fire a third. No one was covering the beefy man and Wayne Brady, engaged with the tall thin man, would have been at his mercy except for a surprise shot from the barn.

Jim Gentry had come out of the barn with only a six-gun. The range was too far for a short-barreled weapon but he fired anyway. His bullet hit nothing, but the sound of gunfire from the barn startled the beefy man and made him miss Brady in his hurry to whirl toward the barn.

Jim was walking this way, still shooting, still out of range and missing. But the diversion of two or three seconds was enough. Before the beefy man could turn back toward Brady, a bullet from Cody's carbine knocked him out of the saddle.

The thin man's horse was snorting, rearing. The man himself was on the ground, not prone but on hands and knees. He was crawling toward a gun which had been jarred from his hand by the fall. Harper was still in the saddle, but bleeding and gunless. He was jerking at his rifle stock, but didn't seem to have strength for pulling it out of the scabbard. Blood on his right sleeve meant a smashed arm bone. His belt gun lay on the ground under his frightened mount.

The beefy man's horse, not the least gunshy, hadn't moved.

By now Jim Gentry was halfway to the bunk cabin and within pistol range. "Did I hit anything?" he called out.

"Only a window pane," Brady told him. There'd been a crash of glass during the shooting. "But you sure spoiled their aim, Jim. Keep 'em covered, Walt, while I pick up their guns."

By the time he'd gathered up all weapons, Jim was with them. A quick look showed that only one of the Brown's Park men had been hit fatally. Harper had only a broken arm. The thin man had a bullet-scratched cheek and a twisted ankle. The shock of the bullet scratch and his plunging horse had toppled him from the saddle, the fall spraining his ankle.

"But this one got it," Jim reported. He was bending over the beefy man, who had a bullet from Walt Cody's rifle in his chest. "Dead-centered," Jim added. In a few minutes more the man had stopped breathing.

Wayne Brady looked toward the main cabin and saw Dale Garrison staring this way. Gunshots from the bunk cabin had drawn him to his front doorway.

"Where they made their mistake," Walt Cody summed up as he used a pigging string to tie the thin man's hands behind his back, "was in not dismounting before they braced us. A man with his feet on the ground can dang near always outgun a man on a horse. The least little move of his horse jars his aim."

Each of the Brown's Parkers had fired one shot. All three bullets were in the door frame; not one of them had touched Wayne Brady or Walt Cody.

"Leaves us with one corpse and two prisoners," Jim remarked. "What do we do with 'em?"

"We take them," Brady decided, "to the court house at Hahn's Peak. Two to the sheriff and one to the coroner."

Cody didn't like it. "And while we're gone," he objected, "Garrison digs up the money and vamooses."

Wayne Brady looked again at the main house and saw Dale Garrison still standing in its open door. "No he won't, Walt. Because he's a witness. An eye witness to fatal gunplay. The only witness who wasn't in the fight—so the coroner needs him more than anyone else at the inquest. We don't leave him here; we take him along with us."

"Will he go?"

"He'll have to," Brady said grimly. "I'm a deputy sheriff, and I'll order him to go as a material witness. Bring in the horse stock, Walt, and start saddling up for the Peak."

It was a ten-mile ride by moonlight, seven horses in single file along a forest trail. Walt Cody, who knew it best, took the lead. Back of him came Jim Gentry, leading the beefy man's horse with a corpse draped across the saddle. Then came the tall, thin man, wrist-bound; then the red-whiskered Harper with a bloody bandage around his gun arm, alternately spewing out moans and cursings. After Harper came Dale Garrison, protesting all the while about being kidnapped. Herding them ahead of him rode Wayne Brady, emergency deputy sheriff of Routt County.

Left alone at the Slater Park ranch was Indian Tom, with no one to cook for but himself. His instructions were simple—he was merely to wait for the return of his master. He could idle there for two or three or four days, shooting ducks, perhaps hooking a trout now and then, and looking after three unused horses. In the moonlight he sat on the masonry coping of a pulley well, sucking a cigaret, well content with his lot—and without the faintest notion that he was sitting on seven thousand dollars stolen from Mark Lassiter.

XVIII

In his Steamboat Springs office, Ambrose Kincaid sat with three newspapers in front of him. They were the latest issues of the two local weeklies and of the Denver *Rocky Mountain News*. All three had the story he wanted most to see. It was a story embellished with exaggerations as new gold strike stories in Colorado always were. Ever since the first gold strike in Gregory Gulch, forty years ago, mineral booms had been the life blood of first the territory and then the state. They drew in people and money. After Gregory Gulch had come Central City, Georgetown, Creede, Leadville, Cripple Creek, and others. Among the very first had been the 1868 strike at Hahn's Peak—a rush which had petered out until almost nothing had been left except a ghostly county seat.

Now here were headlines forecasting its revival. GOLD AGAIN AT THE PEAK! THE FABULOUS JANVERS GULCH RE-DISCOVERED! It was grist to Kincaid's mill, although he knew it wouldn't last long. Right now was the time to cash in before the excitement died down.

Best of all, these three newspapers had still another boom story. It was about plans of the Moffatt line to rush construction toward Salt Lake City via Steamboat Springs and Craig. Mr. Moffatt himself, along with his chief engineer, had just visited Steamboat Springs to scout out a route down the Yampa River. LONGEST TUNNEL IN THE WORLD, read a headline in the *Pilot*. The "Moffatt Tunnel," they'd call it, piercing the great divide to make a fast short route into Routt County.

All of it meant a short ore haul from Hahn's Peak to rails, forecasting that many mines which had been shut down would soon reopen.

So for Kincaid the time was ripe. He unlocked a desk drawer and from it took out a sealed envelope containing three endorsed stock certificates and addressed to the Mining Exchange at

215

Colorado Springs. He went down to the street with it, hurried to the post office, and mailed the envelope.

As he came out, a knot of men were standing on the walk. Their mention of Hahn's Peak drew Kincaid's attention, and he supposed they were talking about the Oliver Creek strike. So he joined them to listen. But no, they were talking about a sensational gunfight at Slater Park. A six-man shootout in which one man had been killed and two wounded.

"Wayne Brady," a teamster was saying, "hustled 'em all to the courthouse. Three Brown's Parkers, one dead and two kicking. Inquest's goin' on right now."

"That's right, Luke. Seems these three guys were all part of a gang with Hix and Wyckes. Which put 'em on a prod agin Brady. They went up there to gun him, but turns out Brady had a pair of siders—Walt Cody and Jim Gentry."

"What about Dale Garrison?" someone asked. "Was he in on it?"

"Not him. But he saw it all. So they took him along as a witness. Doesn't leave anyone there but an Indian cook."

Gunfights at Slater Park didn't interest Kincaid. He went on back to his office.

There he found two clients waiting for him. He'd been expecting them for the last several days. "We drove that rented buckboard of yours down," Benjamin Rumford told him, "and turned it in at the stable."

"We're ready to make you an offer," George Prentiss announced, "for the *Flamingo*."

"How much?" Kincaid asked them.

Rumford produced cigars and passed them around. When they were lighted he sat knee-to-knee with Kincaid and began a down-grading talk. "Look! It's a small creek. Janvers must've skimmed the cream of it ten years ago. The Pomeroys have been grabbing off what's left. Two or three months more work and it's likely to play out. So . . ."

"How much?" Kincaid broke in.

Rumford looked at Prentiss, who cleared his throat to answer. "Ten thousand would be our top offer."

Kincaid gave them a blank stare. "If you want the *Flamingo*, it will cost you twenty-five thousand cash. Take it or leave it."

Rumford threw up his hands. "Ridiculous! We'd never get it back out of that dinky little wash!"

"Then forget it," Kincaid said pleasantly. "I have another bidder on his way here from Aspen. I really oughtn't to sell it at all. My cut from the Pomeroys is running better than five hundred a week—just with shake-panning. When they get to sluicing it should double that." He went to the door and held it open. "Good day, gentlemen."

They got up reluctantly. As they were passing

217

out into the hallway Rumford turned and said: "We've spent a lot of time up there, Kincaid. Don't want to waste it. What about twelve thousand?"

Kincaid smiled and shook his head. "Sorry, gentlemen." After hearing them go down the stairs he sat in his swivel chair, puffing Rumford's cigar, confident that they'd come back again.

They did, an hour later, with an offer of fifteen thousand.

Again Kincaid shook his head—but lowered his price to twenty-two thousand. "Don't forget," he reminded them, "that a new eight-hundred-dollar cabin goes with the claim."

He saw no more of them until late in the afternoon, when they came back with a final offer of eighteen thousand. Convinced that they'd go no higher, Kincaid took it. He endorsed his title to them and accepted Benjamin Rumford's check.

On his way to Milford's bank to deposit it, he saw a tall, black-thatched man with a bony, Lincolnesque face coming toward him along the walk. Nathan Bainbridge.

The sight of Bainbridge made a worry brush Kincaid's mind. A persistent man with a smart head on his shoulders, as attorney for the Lassiter estate he was still nose-down on a hunt for the man or men who'd killed and robbed Lassiter. Where the county lawmen had failed and were still getting nowhere, Bainbridge with his brainy persistence might well succeed.

If he even got a hint of the truth, Kincaid would need to leave Routt County fast—by its back door. Many people would see him if he went by stage to Wolcott. Fewer would see him if he went by saddle on dim wilderness trails to Wyoming.

So on second thought Kincaid changed his mind about depositing his check in Milner's bank. He returned to his office and addressed an envelope to the First National Bank of Rawlins, Wyoming. He wrote a note to the bank directing them to deposit the enclosed check to his account, already established there. Then he sealed the endorsed check, along with his pass book, in the envelope and stamped it. Ten minutes later he'd dropped it in the post office slot.

The inquest at Hahn's Peak had interviewed every witness, and the six jurors were ready with a report.

Deputy Coroner Harris took it from them and read it aloud.

"We find that the deceased, Daniel Hagerman, met his death while feloniously assaulting inmates of a bunk cabin at a ranch in Slater Park; and that said inmates, Walt Cody, Wayne Brady and James Gentry, were forced to defend their lives against the aforesaid assault, initiated and aggravated by the above-mentioned Daniel Hagerman accompanied and supported by Martin Harper and Bernie Burr."

Harris rapped on his desk. "This inquest is adjourned, with the recommendation that Martin Harper and Bernie Burr be charged with attempted murder and held for trial."

The four witnesses, Brady, Cody, Gentry, and Garrison, left the inquest room. Garrison, still complaining for having been brought in to testify, went over to the Hahn's Peak saloon for a drink. The others headed for the stage barn to saddle up.

"What about Garrison?" Cody wondered. "You reckon he'll wanta ride back with us?"

"I figure he will—for two good reasons," Brady said. "He might not be able to find his way back by himself. It's only ten miles—but a dim trail through the woods; it was night time when we came here on it. Top of that, he's got a fat wallet of money on him. His own wad that he drew out of the bank: around three thousand dollars. He got held up for it once, remember? Lots of the wrong kind of people know he's got it."

"So for his own protection," Jim agreed, "he'll want to ride back with us. Even if he *is* mad at us."

Just as they reached the stage barn, an old friend of Brady's came out of it, leading a saddled horse.

The man hailed Wayne eagerly. "Hi, there! You're just the fella I'm lookin' for."

"Howdy, Paul. What the heck are you doing up this way?"

"Came up to record a deed for the boss; and to pay the Two Circle Bar taxes. And look, Wayne, we need you bad for the fall roundup. How about it?"

Brady introduced his friends. "Meet Walt Cody and Jim Gentry. Jim and Walt, this is Paul Dawson, foreman for the Cary brothers down on the Yampa."

As they shook hands all around the Cary foreman looked closely at Jim Gentry. "I remember you, fella. You rode down to the ranch one time to return Brady's wallet that he'd lost up around Shield Mountain."

"Which gives me an idea, Paul," Brady followed up. "You say you need me for the fall roundup—but I can't make it this year. I'm tied up on a county job, and I want to finish it. So why don't you take on Jim in my place?"

Dawson considered it a moment and then nodded. "If Wayne Brady recommends you, that's good enough for me. Okay, Gentry. How soon could you show up?"

"I'm ready to go right now," Jim said quickly. The Two Circle Bar near Hayden was the richest and best-equipped cattle ranch in northwestern Colorado, and the Cary brothers were known to be generous employers. It was often said that beds and food at the cowboy quarters at Cary's

221

were better than could usually be found at the owner's house on other ranches.

"Thanks, Wayne. So long, Walt." Jim saddled up gratefully, and instead of riding to Slater Park he rode south down the stage road with Paul Dawson.

And Brady was right. Dale Garrison came out of the saloon in time to ride to Slater Park with Brady and Cody—rather than try to find his way back alone with three thousand dollars in his wallet.

It was twilight when they got to the ranch and found Indian Tom idling on the well coping, sucking a cigaret.

Walt put up his own mount and Brady's and grained them. When he returned to the bunk cabin, Brady had supper on. "Here we go again, pardner. Two cats and one mouse hole. Which of us stays up all night?"

"Neither of us," Brady decided. "That fella's bushed, after his ride to the Peak and back. Bushed and plenty scared too. First he ran into Wyckes. Next those three Brown's Parkers showed up and began throwing lead. It's going to make him think twice before he heads north with his own money and Lassiter's."

Walt stood in the doorway and looked up at the sky. It was a gray, cloudy sky with a hint of winter in it. "He'll have to make up his mind soon, one way or the other. Here it is September, and I've known it to snow plenty early, this high up. That trail down Slater Creek's likely to be snowed under, month or so from now."

"He's hoping for a break," Brady guessed. "And he almost got one, when Harper and his pals showed up. If they'd downed us, Garrison could have been aboard a train at Rawlins by now."

XIX

Ambrose Kincaid called at the Steamboat Springs post office for his mail. Nothing of importance was there for him that day; nor the next day either. But later in the week what he'd waited for came in.

It was a registered envelope from the Mining Exchange at Colorado Springs. In it was a check for $4164.80—full payment for stock in three mines: the *Tom Thum*, the *Elkhorn*, and the *Minnie D.*

The return more than satisfied Kincaid. Two months ago those blocks of Hahn's Peak stock would have brought much less—in the case of the *Elkhorn*, perhaps nothing at all. The Oliver Creek excitement, plus boom news about the coming of a railroad, had made the difference.

Instead of banking the check, Kincaid decided to keep it in pocket. An official check from the Colorado Mining Exchange was as good as gold

223

and could be promptly cashed at any bank in the West. In his wallet it would be much less bulky than its value in currency. More and more these days, Ambrose Kincaid was thinking in terms of an emergency run-out. He didn't think it would come to that; but it might.

So far there was no breath of suspicion directed his way. Except for Attorney Nathan Bainbridge, he would have felt completely at ease. Bainbridge and his dogged search for a man named Joe.

Kincaid folded the Mining Exchange check and pouched it.

Was there any other loose end to be taken care of? The only one he could think of was his saddle mule up at Hahn's Peak. He remembered an offer he'd had for it once from Reinhart, the Steamboat Springs liveryman. He'd turned it down. The mule was a sure-footed mount for riding rough country up around the Peak.

But a horse would be better, and much less conspicuous, for a sudden, fast, back-door ride out of Routt County.

After mulling it over Kincaid went to the Reinhart stable and dickered for a trade. Reinhart always kept a string of saddle mounts on hand for sale or trade. Kincaid picked the best one in sight and offered to swap his mule for it.

"You think I'm crazy?" the liveryman protested. "I'd need a hundred dollars boot for a deal like that."

"What about fifty?"

They settled for seventy-five dollars boot. Kincaid signed a bill-of-sale for the mule, which Reinhart could pick up at Hahn's Peak whenever he liked, and Reinhart signed a bill-of-sale for the horse. It was a solid bay five-year-old gelding with Morgan blood. Kincaid bought a saddle, bridle, and saddle pad to go with him. "Keep him grained," he told Reinhart. "I'm figuring on a ride up toward Rabbit Ears Pass one of these days."

The ride came sooner than he'd expected, and it wasn't toward Rabbit Ears Pass.

Five days after he'd bought the horse, Kincaid strolled up to the Sheridan Hotel for his midday meal. Two stagecoaches stood in front of it, one northbound for Hahn's Peak and the other southbound for Wolcott. Passengers of both coaches were inside, eating.

Kincaid waited for them to finish so the dining room wouldn't be so crowded. As he idled on the front walk, Nathan Bainbridge and his pretty niece came along and stopped by the Wolcott-bound coach. The lawyer had a travelling bag in hand.

"Goodbye, Uncle Nate." The girl stood on tiptoes to kiss him.

"Take care of yourself, Verna. No telling how long I'll be gone."

Before the lawyer could board the stage, Undersheriff Jack Camp came along and hailed him. "Good luck down there, Mr. Bainbridge."

"Maybe it's a wild goose chase, Jack," the lawyer said, "but it's worth a try. I've drawn a blank everywhere else."

"Give my regards to Mr. Jarbison," Camp said. "He'll remember me from last spring when I took Seb Brobeck to him."

"Okay." Bainbridge promised, and boarded the stage.

When all passengers were aboard, the coach pulled out on its eighteen-hour run to Wolcott.

Two names mentioned by Camp at first alerted, then alarmed Kincaid. The names Jarbison and Brobeck. Earlier this year Brobeck had been sensationally in the headlines. John Eades and Sebron Brobeck had quarreled over Eades' wife, ending in Brobeck's fatal shooting of Eades not two blocks from this hotel. The court at Hahn's Peak had promptly sentenced Brobeck to a life term in the state penitentiary.

With growing alarm Kincaid remembered that a man named Jarbison was warden at that prison.

Put together, it could only mean one thing! At Wolcott Nathan Bainbridge would change to a D. & R. G. train and ride it over Tennessee Pass, on through Leadville and Salida, then through the Royal Gorge to Canon City—site of the Colorado state prison.

Forty-eight hours from now, as surely as death

226

and taxes, Bainbridge would be conferring with Warden Jarbison.

Bainbridge, who for the last several weeks had been persistently searching for someone named Joe! A Joe mentioned with the dying breath of Otto Bundchu! Bundchu who for the last ten years had been an inmate of the Canon City prison!

Bainbridge would be sure to ask the warden for a list of all prisoners named Joe who'd been in the same cell block with Bundchu. And then for permission to interview each one of them.

In which case, sooner or later, he'd inevitably make contact with an ex-cellmate of Bundchu's known as "Little Joe."

A sweat of dread broke out on Kincaid. Here was a hazard he couldn't avert by firing a sneak shot through a window. Little Joe could tell the same tale to Bainbridge that he'd told to Bundchu. A tale about Arizona. Whether they believed him or not, the law would be sure to check with authorities in Arizona. Certainly an inquiry like that would ultimately expose and convict Ambrose Kincaid.

For Kincaid it was a direful warning. If he were to escape, he must get going at once. Not by the front door, which was the direction Bainbridge had just taken and which led squarely through Canon City. The back door of Routt County, through the Elkhead Mountains, the Little Snake Valley to Baggs, thence by stage to Rawlins and the Union Pacific, was the only safe way out.

Once the decision was made, Kincaid lost no time getting ready. Most of his cash assets were already in a Rawlins bank. He could draw out his balance there just before boarding a U.P. train. In his wallet was a gilt-edged check from the Mining Exchange. A modest balance still remained to his credit at the Milner bank here in Steamboat Springs.

Kincaid went there at once and drew it all out except fifty dollars. "To make an investment up around Rabbit Ears," he explained. By leaving fifty dollars in the account, he made it seem that he intended to continue being a depositer here.

At Reinhart's he told them to feed his bay a grain ration and tie two more rations back of his saddle cantle. "A trip up Rabbit Ears way," he told them.

Back in his office, he studied a county map and planned his route. Too many people would see him if he used the Hahn's Peak stage road. He'd need a place to stop and rest himself and his mount. An all-night ride would take him to the Slater Park ranch, where they'd have no reason to suspect him. He knew the situation there: Garrison and an Indian cook in the main house; a deputy sheriff and Walt Cody in the bunk cabin. There'd been a good deal of speculation about it here in Steamboat. On the surface Garrison had merely bought and occupied the Lassiter ranch.

But the clew of a short bridle rein indicated that Garrison had been there on the day of Lassiter's murder, in which case he'd probably rifled Lassiter's money cache and switched the money to a cache of his own. On no other theory would the law have posted two men there to watch Garrison day and night.

No one had more reason to credit that theory than Ambrose Kincaid himself. They must have barely missed each other, that day of Lassiter's death—Kincaid as a killer and Garrison as a thief. And since Kincaid had not picked up the money, that part of the guilt had to be Garrison's.

The price of two hundred mature steers plus Lassiter's earlier savings! It could hardly be less than seven thousand dollars. As Kincaid went to his room at the Onyx Hotel to pack a saddle roll, his mind fixed shrewdly on the Lassiter money. Only Garrison could go to it. But Garrison didn't dare approach it because he was being watched.

Ambrose Kincaid, on his way to Wyoming, would be riding right by there. It was a logical place for him to stop, feeding and resting himself and his mount. Except for the obstacle of two watchers in the bunk cabin, he saw an easy way to get the Lassiter money for himself. A gun punched into Garrison's stomach, with the trigger cocked, should loosen the man's tongue. Lawmen couldn't use a persuader like that; but Kincaid could. Any ruthless killer could. Garrison wouldn't dare deny a cocked gun pushed into his flesh by the same hand which had dealt death to Mark Lassiter.

If only Brady and Cody weren't there, standing by!

Was there a way to get rid of them? Too risky to shoot it out with the two of them. With a silent sigh, Kincaid concluded that he'd have to pass up the bait of the Lassiter money, tempting though it was.

His thoughts reverted to Little Joe, a lifer in the state prison and an ex-cellmate of Otto Bundchu's. Twenty years ago a bartender at Tombstone, Arizona, in the same saloon where Kincaid himself had been a dealer. There had been a tough crowd in that place, some of them outlaws of the Ringo gang, some of them hell-raising cowboys. When one of them became too troublesome, Little Joe, Kincaid recalled, had a way of putting him to sleep. A "knockout drop" in his drink would always do the trick.

It was a knockout which Little Joe had mixed himself. All the floor dealers knew of it, including Kincaid. It had three chemical ingredients, each in itself harmless—but a quick, powerful drug when mixed together.

Concentrating, Kincaid was able to recall those three ingredients. If he had them, he could mix the same knockout himself.

Steamboat Springs had three drugstores—Killon's, Neuman's, and Doctor Solandt's.

In the next hour Kincaid visited them in turn, at each purchasing one of the three ingredients. One was liquid; two were powders. In his Onyx Hotel room he mixed them, pouring the mixture into a four-ounce bottle.

By riding all night he could arrive at the Slater Park ranch in time for breakfast coffee.

Wayne Brady was asleep when Cody looked out, just after dawn, and saw a rider coming from the south. A tall man on a big bay horse. He wasn't wearing a belt gun and his saddle had no scabbarded rifle. Except for the short, pointed beard which gave him a professional look, he might have been a ranch hand on his way to join one of the fall roundups. A light blanket roll was tied back of his saddle.

As the rider came nearer, Cody recognized him. He was a mining broker and consultant with an office at Steamboat Springs and a practice mainly at Hahn's Peak. He knew Ambrose Kincaid only by reputation, and the reputation here in Routt County was as good as anyone's. What was he doing up so early in the morning?

The explanation he gave after dismounting at the cabin might have been true, and Walt Cody had no reason to doubt it. "I had to look up an old prospector over on Circle Creek," the man

231

explained, "and get his signature in order to clear a title for a client of mine. He kept me overnight —but I left at the first crack of daylight so I can meet the client at the Peak."

Circle Creek being only three miles to the southeast, the timetable wasn't unconvincing. No doubt Kincaid had many clients at or near Hahn's Peak; in fact the talk was that he had a rich claim of his own over that way—the *Flamingo*. So to Cody, his passing this way on a ride to the Peak was fairly logical.

"Light and take a load off your saddle," Walt invited.

"What about a feed for my horse? And a spot of coffee for myself?"

"The pot's on and hot; help yourself. I was just going down to the barn to feed my own horse and Brady's; so I might as well take your bay along and stall him for you. You know Wayne Brady, don'tcha?"

Kincaid nodded. "I met him in town once or twice."

As Walt led the bay toward the stable, Kincaid entered the cabin and saw Brady asleep on one of the three bunks. The stove was fired, and there was a coffee pot on it. It might be last night's coffee being reheated for breakfast; or it could be freshly made.

Kincaid poured himself a cup of it. After a furtive look at Brady, he took a four-ounce bottle from an inner pocket and emptied its contents into the pot. He stirred the mixture. That should do it. He set the pot off the stove center so that the coffee wouldn't boil away.

He was seated at the cabin's table sipping his cup of coffee when Cody came back from the barn. "I unsaddled for you, Mr. Kincaid, and put out hay for your bay," he said heartily. Turning to the occupied bunk, he called: "Time to get up, pardner. We got company."

As he swung his legs from the bunk, Brady recognized the visitor as a professional man from Steamboat Springs in good standing. "Hi, there; make yourself at home." His greeting was no less cordial than Cody's.

Walt put bacon in a pan, and by the time Brady was dressed it was crisp and on the table. In a few minutes the three men sat down together. Cody filled his own coffee cup and Brady's, offering to refill Kincaid's. Kincaid accepted the refill, but after that he only pretended to drink. Rolling a cigaret, he said idly, "Understand Dale Garrison bought this place and is living here with an Indian cook."

Cody nodded. "That's right. Yesterday they ran out of flour and spuds, so he sent the cook to Hahn's Peak to stock up. Took along a pack mare and ain't back yet. If you're heading for the Peak this morning, you'll likely meet him on the way."

Kincaid, eyeing them closely, ate the bacon on

his plate and spread jam on a slab of sourdough bread. Brady was on his second cup of coffee and was beginning to look dopey. Again Kincaid pretended to sip from his cup but didn't.

Walt Cody had a stupid look in his eyes and was the first to collapse forward on the table. Wayne Brady gaped at him, mouth hanging open. "Whatsametter, Walt?" He tried to stand up, but his legs wouldn't obey his brain.

He caught the edge of the table to keep from falling. He slumped back into the chair, chin on chest, and in less than a minute more he was out cold.

It was a perfect knockout. Little Joe at his Tombstone bar couldn't have done better. Kincaid dragged Brady to a bunk and toppled him on it, then did the same with Cody. Resting on bunks, they should be out longer he figured—at least six or eight hours. A six-hour start for Kincaid should be enough.

He took the doped coffee pot outside and emptied it. Then he gathered up all firearms in the bunk cabin: two forty-five holster guns and two saddle carbines.

At the main house he'd need to deal only with Garrison. Kincaid headed that way with the four bunk cabin weapons in hand. To get rid of them he dropped them down the pulley well which was midway between the bunk cabin and the main house.

When he got to the house, he tried the front door and found it locked. He circled to the back and looked through a window there. It was the same window through which he'd fired upon Mark Lassiter. Dale Garrison was in there now, standing with his back this way as he spooned grease into a frying pan on the stove.

From an armpit holster Kincaid drew the same gun he'd used on Lassiter.

The kitchen door wasn't bolted. Kincaid, with his gun level, opened it and walked in. As Garrison turned toward him, he stabbed the gun barrel into the man's stomach.

"We're taking a walk, Garrison."

Garrison gave an open-mouth stare. All the blood drained from his face, and for half a minute the shock froze his tongue. Then he gasped out: "A walk? Where?"

"To wherever you hid Lassiter's money."

"Lassiter? I don't know . . . What makes you think . . . ?"

The click as Kincaid cocked the gun stopped him. The muzzle of it punched harder into flesh. "I haven't got much time, Garrison. If you don't want a hole blown through you, you'll start walking toward the money before I count ten. One . . . Two . . . Three . . . Four . . ."

At the count of eight Garrison went into a complete funk and surrendered. "Please . . . I'll split with you . . . you can have half . . ."

"Nine . . . Start walking."

Garrison walked. Stark panic gave wings to his feet as he went outside with a gun barrel boring into his back. Panic made him stumble, and Kincaid had to help him up. Then he circled the house and walked straight toward the stone coping of a well.

XX

Groggily and slowly, Brady came to consciousness—found himself on a bunk, staring at the ceiling, confused, wondering why he'd gone to bed fully dressed, even with his boots on. And why he'd slept so late. And what had given him this splitting headache. He supposed it was early morning; yet it was warm enough to be mid-afternoon.

Then he saw that Cody was on another bunk, also fully dressed and apparently asleep. Even then it was another several minutes before Brady realized it wasn't a question of oversleeping. He looked at the table and saw breakfast plates; used plates; three of them. Hadn't Walt washed the supper dishes? In any case, there should be only two.

"Walt!" He called the name thickly; there was no answer.

Then he remembered a breakfast guest. A Steamboat Springs man with a short, pointed beard. Not an overnight guest. He'd arrived at sunup on a big bay horse. He'd joined them for bacon and coffee. . . .

Brady sat up and got his feet on the floor. His head was still pounding, but he could think now. This wasn't the first time he'd gotten up today. It was the second time. That clock on the window sill told him that it was two hours past noon.

"Walt!" He crossed to the other bunk and shook Cody.

He had to shake Cody twice before he looked up with heavy-lidded eyes. Brady shook him again. "He tricked us, Walt; put us to sleep, some way." But he didn't mean Ambrose Kincaid. Only Dale Garrison would do this. Garrison, who'd been matching wits with them for weeks, waiting his chance—hoping to get them off guard so that he could reclaim hidden money and run with it.

Brady filled a wash pan with cold water and swabbed his face. He soaked a rag and slapped it over Cody's face. "On your feet, Walt, while I go to the house and see if he's gone."

He turned toward a wall peg where he'd hung his cartridge belt and gun. The belt was there, but the gun was gone. The gun was missing from Walt's belt too. Two saddle carbines should be standing in a corner. They weren't there. It all fit with a runout. Naturally the man would take away all the bunk cabin guns so that pursuers would be left unarmed.

237

His mind still on Garrison, and still unable to connect what had happened with anyone but Garrison, Wayne Brady went out and headed at an unsteady run toward the house. Halfway there, something brought him to an abrupt stop. One of the stones of the masonry well coping had been removed and now lay to one side. The removal exposed a rectangular cavity about the size and shape of a cigar box. On the ground nearby, open and empty, lay a metal box of that size and shape.

The money box! Here then was where Garrison had hidden the Lassiter money! Early this morning he must have taken it and made off, after first doping . . .

But had he? Was it Garrison who'd made off? As his brain cleared, Brady began to have second thoughts. Someone beyond any doubt had doped the breakfast coffee. In no other way could both Brady and Cody have been put to sleep. Yet how could Garrison have done that? He hadn't been there. Only Kincaid had been there. Kincaid, claiming to have been on his way to Hahn's Peak.

Brady hurried on to the house. The front door was locked, but the back door wasn't. He went inside and found that a breakfast fire had been made in the kitchen stove. A frying pan had melted grease in it. Someone had started to make breakfast here and had been interrupted. The house was empty. Garrison's bed had been slept in, but the man was gone.

What about horses? Last night there'd been two horses in the corral. A third, Kincaid's, had arrived early this morning. Brady hurried down there and saw that all three animals were missing. His own horse, Garrison's, and Kincaid's. Cody's mount as well as one belonging to Mark Lassiter should be out in the pasture. Indian Tom, riding a horse and leading a grub-laden pack mare, should be on the way back from Hahn's Peak.

Brady went to the bunk cabin and found Cody with his face buried in a pan of cold water. "He took our guns, Walt. And our horses; left us afoot."

Walt looked up with a dopey stare. "You mean Garrison?"

"It could be Garrison. More likely it was Kincaid. Or maybe they're in cahoots. When Garrison was in Steamboat Springs, he could have rigged it up with Kincaid—offered him a split if he'd come by here and put us to sleep."

"Which way did they go?" Walt muttered, still with a stupid stare.

"They, or he," Brady reasoned, "wouldn't go to Hahn's Peak. That'd be straight toward the sheriff and the county jail. Nor back to Steamboat Springs. His or their best chance for a getaway would be to head north for Rawlins and the first fast U.P. train."

Walt looked at the clock, shook his head to get the cobwebs out of it, and saw that it was past two in the afternoon. "They've got an eight-hour start," he said dismally.

Brady led him to the well and pointed out the moved coping stone and the empty money box. "The more I think of it, Walt, the more I think Kincaid did it all by himself. Nobody else had a chance to dope us."

Cody's wits were more than halfway back by now. "Kincaid, huh? Maybe he's the guy who sneaked up here and shot Lassiter."

"In which case he's a cold killer," Brady added. "A cold killer wouldn't split with Garrison. He'd gun Garrison and take everything in sight."

On that possibility they searched the house, barn, sheds and grounds, more than half expecting to find Dale Garrison's body. When they didn't, Brady revised his conclusions.

"Let's say he knocked us out, Walt, then went up to the house and put a gun on Garrison. He could make Garrison lead him to the money, then whang down on the guy; maybe he killed him, or maybe he just knocked him cold. But if we should find Garrison that way, we'd know for sure that Kincaid had raided us. With Garrison missing, we might think he made off with the money while Kincaid had gone innocently on to Hahn's Peak. Which is what we *did* think at first."

Cody tried to find a hole in it, but couldn't. "Okay," he agreed, "so he takes Garrison along with him, dead or alive, draped across a saddle;

then ditches him in a thicket a mile or so down the trail, heading on by himself for Rawlins."

"Let's play it that way, Walt. He has an eight-hour start, so we won't be able to catch up with him. By the time we get to Rawlins, he'll likely have left there by train. But we can have the Rawlins sheriff wire both ways along the line and have him grabbed either at Salt Lake City or Cheyenne, depending on which way he goes."

Walt pointed east. "We ain't quite afoot, either. There comes Indian Tom from the Peak with a packload of grub."

When the cook rode up, Walt commandeered his mount and used it to wrangle in his own horse from pasture. It gave them two mounts, one jaded and one fresh. Cody grained and saddled them both.

By shortly after three o'clock he was riding with Brady down the Slater Creek trail. It was little used now, but likely to become an important beef trail for the Elkhead Mountains ranches, once the Moffatt line pushed its rails to Steamboat Springs.

"The Reverse 4," Brady remembered, "has a line camp about ten miles downcreek from here. Maybe they'll give us some fresh mounts."

"Which won't help much," Walt muttered. "Kincaid'll be dang near to Baggs by then."

"But he'll be too late," Brady calculated, "to catch today's stagecoach from Baggs to Rawlins."

"There's a livery stable at Baggs, Wayne. Nothin' to stop him from hiring a rig, him with a pocketful of money. By drivin' all night he could hit Rawlins by sunup tomorrow."

They rode on another mile, following the twists of the creek with willow brush to the left and a piny slope to the right. Suddenly a sound made Brady rein up abruptly. It seemed to be a moan of distress from a thicket of willows.

When they looked in the thicket, they found Dale Garrison with a bleeding skull and only a breath of life left in him.

Even when Cody bathed the man's face with cold creek water, they couldn't revive him enough for speech.

"The way it looks," Cody guessed, "Kincaid socked him, then put him across a horse and led the horse this far so we wouldn't find him too soon. Right here Kincaid ditched him. By riding on alone leading Garrison's horse, he has a remount."

"He can shift from saddle to saddle," Brady agreed glumly, "and keep widening the gap."

"So what do we do?"

"We can't leave Garrison here to die," Brady decided. "Besides, we need him for a witness. So I'll push along to Rawlins by myself. You put Garrison on your horse and take him back to the ranch. Do what you can for him while Tom rides for a sheriff and a doctor."

"Get going," Walt agreed.

Riding on alone, Brady made the Reverse 4 line camp by five o'clock. Only one herder and a cook were there, but more riders were expected, and the corral had a few remounts. Brady borrowed one and shifted his saddle to it. "Did a man pass here this morning heading downcreek, riding a bay and leading a sorrel? Tall man in corduroys with a short pointed beard."

The line camp herder shook his head. "Nobody passed here all day, Brady."

"Means he detoured you to keep from being seen," Brady concluded. "It'd make him lose maybe twenty minutes. Thanks." He rode on astride the borrowed horse, leading his own.

Columbus Mountain loomed to the right with Sawtooth on the left. In the next few miles he sighted a bunch of Reverse 4 steers and a band of OVO mares. He pushed off and at the mouth of Beaver Creek saw a rider coming his way. He was Jess Finnegan of the OVO and Brady had been on roundups with him. "Hi, Jess," Brady said. "I'm chasing a fella named Kincaid. Know him? A Steamboat Springs mining man; wears a short pointed beard and rides a big bay. He's leading a sorrel. Did you pass him?"

"I sure did, Brady. About noon just this side of the Slater post office. What's he done?"

"My hunch is he shot Mark Lassiter; plenty of other devilment on top of that. Stop at the Lassiter ranch when you get there and talk to Walt Cody.

Give Walt all the help you can, Jess. If anybody asks you, I'm heading for the U.P. telegraph office at Rawlins."

Jess promised to stop at Slater Park, and Brady rode on, his eyes searching the trail for hoof marks of Kincaid's two horses. He couldn't make them out because too many range cattle had crossed here.

Further on he came to open country where sheep had grazed the grass short. It allowed him to see something which high grass would have hidden. It seemed to be an article of black leather, about four inches by six, lying a few yards off the trail.

When Brady dismounted and picked it up, he saw that it was a man's wallet. Whatever money had been in it was gone; but a few cards and receipts identified the wallet as Dale Garrison's.

Nor did finding it here surprise Brady. Kincaid, after cracking down on Garrison, would of course take his wallet. A fat haul in itself, because Garrison was known to have drawn three thousand dollars from the Milner bank on his last trip to town. Kincaid would pocket the wallet. Later, after several hours of travel made him feel safely away, he'd take time to strip the money from the wallet and throw the wallet away.

Brady put it in his own pocket and rode on.

He made the U Bar in time for supper; they gave him coffee and a plate of beans. This was the ranch which had promised Jim Gentry a job and later turned him down. They hadn't seen Kincaid pass. Brady rode on in deep twilight. It was eight o'clock and dark when he forded the Little Snake and drew up at the Slater post office.

He described Kincaid to the Slater postmistress.

"Yes," she said, "a man like that came by here just after noon. He asked how far it was to Baggs, and I told him about fourteen miles."

The post office was also a wayside store, and Brady bought two rations of grain. He fed both mounts, rested them briefly, and rode on toward Baggs. Less than a mile beyond Slater he crossed the state line into Wyoming. The little store at Savery, Wyoming, was dark when he passed it. He changed horses and pushed on. It was midnight when he pulled up at the Baggs livery stable.

He wakened the liveryman and asked about Kincaid. "Yeh, he left both his mounts here and hired a two-horse rig. Said he had a business deadline at Rawlins and needed to get there fast."

Brady had often been in Baggs and knew the liveryman quite well. "You rented him a rig, Harry?"

"Why not? He paid in advance and left his own two horses here till he gets back."

Brady took a look at the horses, a bay and a sorrel, and saw that they'd been pushed hard. They wouldn't have been able to go the sixty miles to Rawlins without a long rest.

"The man's a killer, Harry. I've got to get some telegrams off both ways along the U.P. So I'll need a rig myself—the best two-horse team you've got for a fast drive to Rawlins."

XXI

Harry the Baggs liveryman not only rented Wayne Brady his best two-horse rig, he furnished a driver as well. "So you can get some sleep on the way, Brady. You look like you need it."

"It's a sixty-mile run," the driver said as he trotted his team north out of Baggs. "I figure it'll take Kincaid fourteen hours. We can make it in ten and gain four hours on him."

"How's that?" Brady looked in surprise at the driver, an old stagecoach hand named McCoy.

"First place, we've got a better team. Second place, we'll change to fresh horses three times, at the regular stage line relay stations."

"Why can't Kincaid do the same thing?"

"Because the relay stations'll turn him down. They won't turn us down because I've got an order from Harry. Harry owns a third interest in this Rawlins-Baggs-Craig-Meeker stage line. Better lean back now and get some sleep." McCoy cracked his whip, pushing his span of blacks to a run.

"Just one question," Brady said. "Long time since I've seen a Union Pacific schedule. When do the trains go through Rawlins?"

"Two trains a day each way. Eastbound local goes through at 9:22 a.m. Eastbound express goes through at 8:10 p.m. Westbound local goes through at 2:30 a.m. Westbound express goes through at 10:55 a.m."

Fumbling for a pad and pencil in the starlight, Brady made a note of the schedules. A few minutes later he was fast asleep.

He wasn't aware of the stop to change horses at the first relay station. They were pulling out of the second relay station, Sulphur Springs on Muddy Creek, when Brady opened his eyes and saw that it was after daybreak.

Driver McCoy's fresh team was at a trot. "We've already gained two hours on that bugger," he boasted. "He left Sulphur with a tired team at one a.m. If he tries to force 'em faster than a walk they'll play out on him. Be seven o'clock before he gets to Rawlins."

"And when," Brady asked, "will we get there?"

"We oughta make it by ten—only three hours behind him. Giddap." McCoy whipped his team to a trot.

Brady took out his train schedule and looked at it. "First train he can catch," he concluded, "will be the eastbound local at 9:22. Next one'd be the westbound express at 10:55."

As he put the note pad back in his pocket, his fingers touched the rifled billfold he'd picked up on the Slater Creek trail—the one Kincaid had tossed aside after stripping money from it.

In the press of yesterday's pursuit Brady had examined it only long enough to make sure it was Garrison's. Now, at his leisure, he looked through it in detail. There was a receipt for room rent at the Sheridan Hotel; another receipt for one thousand dollars made as a down payment on the Slater Park ranch; and a card or two of no consequence.

But a separate compartment of the wallet had a small, sealed envelope. The outside of the envelope was blank. Brady opened it curiously and found a penned message. It said:

In case of my death by violence, please send the following telegrams:

First National Bank
Hartford, Connecticut:
    Homer Wilcox is living at Steamboat Springs, Colorado, as Abner Barnett:

J. Jones.

Charles St. Charles
Beacon Hill, Boston, Mass.
    Your wife is living at Steamboat Springs, Colorado, as Mrs. Abner Barnett.

J. Jones.

Brady blinked at the telegrams, as yet unsent; he read them again and again. By the time he'd reached the third and last relay station on the stage road to Rawlins, the entire masquerade of Dale Garrison at Steamboat Springs had become clear to him. He'd gone there not to buy a stock ranch but to prey on the town's leading merchant. The source of a one-thousand-dollar quarterly income was no longer a mystery. Some time in the past Homer Wilcox, now calling himself Abner Barnett, had absconded with bank money and another man's wife.

Brady put the messages back in the wallet and restored the wallet to his pocket. He'd let Sheriff Farnham at Steamboat deal with them. Today Brady himself would be busy dealing with Ambrose Kincaid.

At exactly ten o'clock McCoy drove across the tracks at Rawlins and a block beyond, at the corner of Fifth and Cedar, stopped at the county jail. If Kincaid had left on the eastbound local, and the local was on time, he would have cleared the town thirty-eight minutes ago.

In that case a telegram to authorities at Cheyenne, a hundred and fifty miles east of here, should stop him.

Brady took a deputy's badge from his pocket and pinned it on his jacket. It gave him no authority in this Wyoming county, but it would serve as an introduction to the local sheriff. He hit the sidewalk almost as soon as the rig stopped and was fortunate enough to find Sheriff Pixlee of Carbon County at his desk.

"Listen, Sheriff, we're short of time and I'll have to talk fast. I'm from Routt County, across the line. Chased a killer all the way here. Tall dark man with a pointed beard named Kincaid. Wears corduroys and a cowman's hat. He may have caught the 9:22 local east; or be waiting for the 10:55 express west. We've got to nail him."

Pixlee looked at Brady's badge and then at his gunless waist. "You're the first manhunter I ever saw," he said, "without a gun on."

"He doped me and took away my gun," Brady explained. "I can tell you the rest of it on the way to the depot. We'd better hurry."

"Who did he kill?"

"Mark Lassiter for one; in Slater Park last month."

"I heard about it. Let's go."

As they started out, Pixlee took a gunbelt from a wall peg. Its holster had a gun in it. "Better put this on, fella, in case he's on the depot platform and starts shooting. What did you say your name is?"

"Brady."

Out on the sidewalk Brady spoke to the Baggs driver, McCoy. "Put the rig up at a livery barn and then check all local barns to see if Kincaid turned in his own outfit. If he didn't he must have left it at a street hitchrail. Then report to us at the depot."

Pixlee and Brady headed east along Cedar Street, past the town's two banks and the leading stores. In rapid fire words Brady gave the sheriff a few more details. Pixlee listened grimly, without comment.

At the corner of Fourth Street they ran into the Rawlins town constable, idly patrolling. The sheriff beckoned him. "Better come along with us, Kim."

Kim joined them, and they turned south on Fourth, passing by the Maxwell Hotel. Half a block further they came to the Union Pacific depot. The platform was deserted. A day operator was on duty at the track-front bay window.

Pixlee conferred with him briefly and then rejoined Brady on the platform. "The eastbound local was on time," he reported. "Five people boarded it here, but they were all Rawlins folk, well-known to the operator. He says he saw no stranger."

"Means our man's holed up somewhere in town," Brady concluded, "waiting for the westbound express."

The sheriff looked at his watch. "Due in forty minutes. I'll wait here and keep my eyes open." He turned to the constable. "Meantime, Kim, you better check the hotels and rooming houses.

We're looking for a tall dark stranger in corduroys and a cowman's hat; has a short, pointed beard. He hit town about three hours ago and would want to keep out of sight till train time."

The constable hurried off.

"When did the stores open?" Brady asked.

"Eight o'clock. Why?"

"If I were in his place I'd want to buy a new suit and hat. Something different from a tall Stetson and corduroys."

The sheriff nodded. "Try the James France store and then Granger's. They're both on the main street. And you'd better get back here by train time."

Brady hurried up to Cedar Street and went in turn to the town's two largest general stores. At one he drew a blank. At the other he got the right answer. "Sure," the head clerk told him. "Man like that came in just as we opened at eight o'clock. Bought a blue serge business suit and a center-creased fedora. Also a small handbag. Fastest sale I ever made. He was gone by half past eight."

"Which direction?"

"I didn't notice."

Brady went out and looked both ways along the street. In a moment he saw the Baggs driver, McCoy, coming toward him along the walk. "I found his rig," McCoy reported. "He hit town at seven o'clock and left it at Newt Rankin's stable."

"Okay," Brady said. "An hour later he bought a

252

new suit and hat. That still left him two hours and a half till train time. Where could he keep out of sight?"

"What about barbershops," McCoy suggested. "Three of 'em in town. He could kill an hour getting that beard shaved off; after that maybe a hot towel face massage and a hot bath. He could lay doggo in a barbershop bathtub till train time."

"Check the barbershops," Brady directed.

The Baggs driver nodded. "And while I'm doing that, maybe you'd better check the banks."

"The banks? Why?"

"When he put up his team he asked the liveryman what time the banks open. The liveryman said ten o'clock."

There were two banks, both on this street, one in midblock, the other at the corner of Fourth. Brady considered them shrewdly. You go into a bank for one of two reasons: either to put money in or take it out. Kincaid in flight wouldn't make a deposit—but he might make a withdrawal. Being on the wrong side of the law he could have prepared this route of escape a long time in advance.

A logical preparation, Brady reasoned, would be to salt away the bulk of his money in a Rawlins bank, ready to be withdrawn just before boarding a getaway train. It would explain why he hadn't left on the 9:22 local. The banks didn't open till ten o'clock, and he'd need to wait for the first train leaving after that hour.

It was now 10:27—twenty-eight minutes before train time. Brady walked by both banks and looked in. Kincaid wasn't in either. The bank theory began to look thin. Yet why would the man inquire when the banks opened unless he planned to call at one of them?

If he did, it would have to be in the next few minutes. Brady posted himself about halfway between the two banks—the Carbon County Bank and the First National. He stood with his back against a saloon front and watched alertly in both directions.

The street was quiet. Here and there a ranch rig or a cow pony was tied at a hitchrail. A few women shoppers passed. A boy was sweeping off the sidewalk in front of the Rasmussen store. Two stock hands cantered up, tied their mounts, and went into a saloon across the street.

At 10:34 a tall, clean-shaven man rounded the corner from Fifth. He wore a blue serge suit and a center-creased fedora, and he carried a small satchel. If he hadn't been alert for such a change, Brady might not have recognized him. But he was Ambrose Kincaid, all right.

Kincaid, fresh from a barbershop where he'd kept out of sight for most of the last two hours!

If the man wore a gun it wasn't exposed anywhere. Brady walked slowly toward him. He was a bare twenty paces away when the man began turning into the First National Bank.

Brady called sharply: "That's far enough, Kincaid. Couple of sheriffs looking for you, not counting me. If you've got any money in that bank you'll have to leave it right there."

The man in the blue serge suit snapped toward him, his hand darting to a hidden armpit holster. His gun was out before Brady could draw his own, and his bullet beat Brady's by a breath. Both draws were too fast for accuracy at that range, and both bullets missed. It was Brady who got off the first second shot. It hit Kincaid's right shoulder and spun him half around. The spin made his next shot go wild, and Brady didn't let him have a third one.

All the time he'd been walking toward the man, and he was only about twelve steps away when his third bullet hit Kincaid's middle chest and dropped him on the bank walk.

Men came running from shops, saloons, banks. The shots and the shouting drew McCoy from his round of barbershops and Constable Kim from his round of hotels. Sheriff Pixlee, puffing hard, came on a run from the depot; finally a doctor looked at Ambrose Kincaid and pronounced him dead.

A cashier came out of the bank and recognized him. "He opened an account with us a year ago, and just last week he sweetened it with an eighteen-thousand-dollar deposit."

"He's got another good-size check in his wallet," Pixlee reported after a look. "For forty-six hundred dollars signed by the Colorado Mining Exchange. And a big wad of cash."

Most of the cash, Brady informed them, belonged to the estate of Mark Lassiter.

From up the track to the east, a westbound train whistled. The Omaha-to-San-Francisco express. It came pounding in, stopped at the Rawlins depot, changed engines, and was soon speeding onward toward the Pacific coast.

"Except for you," Sheriff Pixlee said grimly to Wayne Brady, "he'd be on it."

Brady hardly heard him. He was weary to the edge of collapse. The pursuit from Slater Park had been more than a hundred miles, and all he wanted now was a hot bath and a long sleep. After that, a quiet, leisurely journey back to Slater Park, and Steamboat Springs, and Verna Bainbridge.

XXII

It was two weeks later, and the first early fall snow fluttered down: a warmish wet snow of which each flake melted as it hit the ground. Cottonwoods along the Yampa River still had leaves. Traffic on Steamboat Springs' main street was no different from yesterday, except that women shoppers wore overshoes and men wore leather jackets or sheepskin coats. Horses at the hitchrails stood patiently, heads dropped.

What passed for a stagecoach pulled out, not southbound for Wolcott or northbound for Hahn's Peak, but westbound down the river for Hayden and Craig.

The downriver stage wasn't a big nine-passenger Concord, like the ones on the Wolcott run. This one was only a narrow-tired spring wagon with a canvas top. And today there were only two passengers. Their tickets were to Hayden, twenty-odd miles down the river. Round trip tickets. They were a young man and a young woman. The young woman wore a heavy woolen coat and a fur neckpiece, a laprobe covering her knees. It was just cold enough to bring a bright pink to her cheeks. A hood came down over her ears. The man wore a plaid mackinaw with a turned-up collar. His arm was looped loosely around the girl's shoulders.

Knowing this, the driver very rarely looked back at them. But he talked almost incessantly.

"Understand you're gonna dab down on the Dave Gibbs place," he suggested.

"That's up to Verna," Wayne Brady told him.

"I getcha. You figure to show her the house and see if she'd like to live there."

"I'm sure I will." This time the answer came from Verna Bainbridge.

"It's a right nice quarter section," the driver

volunteered. "I orter know, seein' as I drive by there six times a week. Level as a pool table. All meadow, right on the riverbank. Four-room rock house. Needs fixin', maybe. Ain't nobody lived there since the Gibbses went back east."

He whipped his team to a trot, and for a while there was no sound except the clop-clop of hooves.

Then, "How come you don't take the Lassiter place, up in Slater Park? It's back on the market, I hear," he said.

"Because eight thousand feet's too high," Brady explained, "for a man who hopes to raise a family. No schoolhouse up that way. Too long a winter and too short a summer."

"What you reckon they'll do to that fella Garrison?" the driver wondered. "They tell me he's gonna pull through."

"He'll be charged with blackmail and tried in the Hahn's Peak court."

"What about grand larceny? Didn't he steal Mark Lassiter's money?"

This time Verna answered. "According to Uncle Nate, he didn't. All he did was fail to report finding it. We think he found the money but didn't touch it. He planned to steal the money later, but Wayne and Walt never gave him a chance."

"I getcha. It was Kincaid who swiped that wad, huh? Put a gun on Garrison and made him tell where it was. What did your uncle find out about that fella, Miss Verna, when he got to Canon City?"

"Not a thing," Verna said. "He found a prisoner named Little Joe who'd been a cellmate of Otto Bundchu's. But Little Joe wouldn't admit anything."

"The prison warden," Brady explained, "says that hard cases like Little Joe generally won't give out anything to the law. Just as Mr. Bainbridge was about to give up, he got my telegram from Rawlins telling about how we'd run down Kincaid there. So Mr. Bainbridge asked Little Joe what he knew about Kincaid. Joe still wouldn't spill anything, but he'd look sly and secretive every time Kincaid's name was mentioned. Whatever he knows he's keeping to himself."

"So it's a good thing you took care of him at Rawlins," the driver said. "No way to prove he ever killed anybody. If he was alive, all they could pin on him'd be his doping of you and Walt Cody that day, whangin' down on Garrison and makin' off with the dough."

"That's all," Brady agreed.

"What about Abner Barnett?"

"He's on his way back to Connecticut, charged with embezzling eighty thousand dollars of bank money three or four years ago."

Again there was a silent interval as the driver let his team walk for a mile. They came to the wayside village of Milner. Verna raised her hooded head from Brady's shoulder while they passed a livery stable, a blacksmith shop, and a store–post office, and while the driver tossed off one mail sack and took on another. When they cleared the village the girl's head settled back to the same resting place and the man's arm tightened snugly about her shoulders.

Presently the driver thought of something else. "They say an insurance company had to cough up that eighty thousand; so now they've grabbed Ab Barnett's Steamboat Springs property to get even. It's the insurance company that's payin' you the reward, ain't it? Enough to buy the Dave Gibbs place with?"

"Enough for a down payment," Brady said.

The driver chuckled. "All because you were lucky enough to pick up Garrison's wallet with them two telegrams in it. How much prison time do you reckon they'll give Barnett?"

Brady didn't hazard a guess. A flurry of snow came in under the canvas top and spanked against his face. He drew the laprobe higher around Verna.

Another few miles brought them to a change station at the mouth of Wolf Creek. A relay team was ready and was soon hooked on. The warm wet flakes were still falling. The driver cracked his whip and pushed the fresh horses to a trot.

He was still talkative and curious. "What

about the woman Barnett ran away with? A Mrs. St. Charles? They gonna arrest her too?"

"I don't think so," Brady said. "She's still in Steamboat Springs."

The driver shook his head sadly. "I kinda feel sorry for that lady—her husband not wantin' to take her back and Barnett snatched off to jail leavin' her alone and busted there."

The narrow-tired stagecoach rattled on down the river road. Soon the valley widened into fenced hay meadows with clusters of stacks here and there.

Wayne Brady pointed ahead to neatly painted white buildings—an imposing ranch head-quarters. "The Cary brothers place, Verna. Biggest spread in the county. Controls fifty thousand acres and runs five thousand cows. Jim Gentry took my job there. The Gibbs homestead is just a piece beyond it."

They drove on by the Cary ranch and presently came to a little roadside country schoolhouse with a bell in its cupola. It was quiet and deserted, today being Saturday with no school in session.

Across from it a plank gate had the name Gibbs on it. Beyond the gate they could see a small rock house with a well and outsheds. This was the quarter section of fenced level meadow which reached from the stage road to cottonwoods lining the Yampa River. Vern's first sight of it was through a curtain of falling snow.

The driver stopped his rig at the gate, and Brady helped Verna out. The snow still melted as it fell but the air had turned colder.

"You'll pass the upriver stage at Hayden?" Brady asked the driver. The little cattle town of Hayden was only four miles downriver.

"Yep. We both change horses there. Want me to tell it to stop here and pick you up?"

"Please," Brady said. "That gives us about two hours to look the place over."

The driver nodded. "I've seen folks start housekeepin' in worse places than this." He thumbed toward the schoolhouse. "A handy place to send your kids," he said to Verna, and drove on.

About the Author

Allan Vaughan Elston was a prolific author of traditional Western novels and many more short stories and novelettes, memorable for the complexity of their plots and the flamboyance of the villains who are often more interesting than either the heroes or heroines. He was born in Kansas City and spent his summers on a Colorado cattle ranch owned by his father. He was educated as a civil engineer at the University of Missouri and worked in various engineering companies in South America as well as his own in the United States before, in 1920, turning to ranching. Times were hard financially at the ranch so in late 1924 Elston tried writing his first fiction. His first story was "The Eyes of Teconce" in *The Frontier* (2/25), an adventure tale set in the rugged Andes, but his second was "Peepsight Shoots High" in *The Frontier* (6/25), marking his debut as an author of Western fiction, in which henceforth he specialized. His second Western story was "Triggers in Leash" in *The Frontier* (7/25), subsequently adapted for the third episode of "Alfred Hitchcock Presents" in 1955. His first Western novel was *Come Out and Fight!* (1941) followed by *Guns on the Cimarron* (1943) prior to his re-entering the U.S. Army during the Second

World War. Following the war, he found his stride with *Hit the Saddle* (1947) and *The Sheriff of San Miguel* (1949). In the 1950s he would average two books a year, an impressive accomplishment for any writer and Elston was already into his sixties. His novels tend to be precisely situated as to year and place and often contain an intriguing mystery. *The Landseekers* (1964) was Elston's final novel to appear in a hard cover edition. Henceforth, he confined himself to writing paper-back originals. At his best, Elston was a fine craftsman who could unite novelty of setting and events with a plot-driven complexity to produce a generally entertaining narrative.

Center Point Large Print
600 Brooks Road / PO Box 1
Thorndike, ME 04986-0001 USA

(207) 568-3717

US & Canada:
1 800 929-9108
www.centerpointlargeprint.com